"Hunt, what is it going to take to get through to you on this?

I own this property. Temple Territory is going to become Moore House. You can roll with the punches or punch out. I will meet my opening deadline, with or without you. So which will it be?"

Hunt folded his arms, did an about-face and seemed to study something outside the window. His white knit shirt stretched tight across solid shoulders, revealing the body of a man who could have played professional baseball—if everybody who ever mentioned him to her was to be believed. Those powerful arms could definitely swing a bat.

Or hold a woman close.

Maybe she'd been hasty. What if he walked away? She'd be out more than an executive chef.

Oh, knock it off. Don't let your emotions get in the way of your plans.

"Well, what's it going to be?"

Dear Reader,

"In the great oilfield piracy trials of 1960, many were tried, many were sued, many faced a jury, many heard the prosecutors condemn them as thieves and crooks and pirates. But no one went to jail. No one went to prison....When it came time for a jury of twelve good men to make a decision that would forever affect the lives of their community, they no longer talked about the thieves and crooks and pirates. They felt a close kinship with a bunch of good, hard-working, and unfortunate neighbors, businessmen, and church deacons who weren't guilty of anything but hauling out a little black gold that the Good Lord had put in the earth."–Author Caleb Pirtle III

As an oil-well survey engineer and witness for the prosecution, my father was part of the trial proceedings mentioned above. Daddy told me stories of being chaperoned by a Texas Ranger, sitting in local restaurants with his back to the wall and his face to the door and of having his expert testimony challenged on the witness stand as if he were the one on trial for oil piracy. In the end, no one went to prison for the crimes committed against the major oil companies. But my daddy's memories fueled my writer's hunger to tell a "what if" story about the lives of brothers, two generations later, who'd grown up in a small East Texas town in the shameful shadow of their grandfather's scapegoat conviction.

My Deep in the Heart series is about brothers Hunt, Cullen, Joiner and McCarthy Temple. Each brother, in his own way, struggles with their family history and, in his own way, rises above the past to create a life and future worthy of the Lone Star State. Please enjoy Hunt's story, *Cowboy in the Kitchen*.

Until we meet again, let your light shine!

Mae Nunn

HARLEQUIN HEARTWARMING

Mae Nunn

Cowboy in the Kitchen

Deep in the Heart

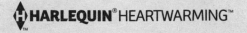

Recycling programs
for this product may
not exist in your area.

ISBN-13: 978-0-373-36647-7

COWBOY IN THE KITCHEN

Copyright © 2013 by Mae Nunn

Printed in U.S.A.

www.Harlequin.com

MAE NUNN

grew up in Houston and graduated from the University of Texas with a degree in communications. When she fell for a transplanted Englishman living in Atlanta, she moved to Georgia and made an effort to behave like a Southern belle. But when she found that her husband was quite agreeable to life as a born-again Texan, Mae happily returned to her cowgirl roots and cowboy boots! In 2008 Mae retired from thirty years of corporate life to focus on her career as a full-time author.

This book is for my daddy, Ward Cooper, whose life experiences inspired me to create the Deep in the Heart series. And it's also for my aunt, Lucille Cooper Perry, who inspired me to keep writing when I was quite happy to rest on my laurels. Daddy and Aunt Lucille, you are each amazing in your own right, and I thank God that I still have both of you in my life.

CHAPTER ONE

GILLIAN MOORE STOOD between Hunt Temple and the morning sun of a cool September day as effectively as she stood between him and his heritage. It wasn't enough that she'd cast a shadow across his life by purchasing his grandfather's estate, she had to block his reading light, too. Hunt's quiet moments on the back steps of what was once Pap's home had come to an end.

Possibly for the last time.

"Would you mind if I join you?" she asked.

Without waiting for his response, the lady gracefully folded her tall, slender body to perch on the edge of the step nearby. She shrugged off the shoulder strap of a glitzy red-leather handbag and settled it beside her on the fieldstone ledge—where she had not been asked to have a seat.

But as the property's future owner she hardly required his invitation.

Slanted rays of East Texas sunlight glinted off her fancy dark glasses. Even a guy like Hunt, who'd spent most of his life in a kitchen, recognized the pricey logo on the rich-girl shades. Besides, he'd noticed it splashed all over Paris during his recent trip to visit old friends at Le Cordon Bleu.

The attractive woman offered a smile his way that he might find charming under different circumstances. Instead of returning it, Hunt lowered his gaze to check out her long bare legs. French manicured toenails were poking through high-heeled sandals that she'd pulled close to the step beneath them. She tugged at the hem of her knee-length skirt and sat with her spine ramrod straight, expectant as a high-strung bird dog waiting on shotgun fire.

She was uncomfortable. Good.

"It's lovely, isn't it?" Her question was rhetorical, just something to break the silence.

"I've always thought so," he responded anyway. "Since I was old enough to drive,

I've been coming to this spot to enjoy the quiet. *Alone*."

"I'm sorry to interrupt," she apologized. "But I didn't expect anyone to be here, Mr. Temple."

"Mr. Temple was my grandfather," he corrected her. "Mason Dixon Temple to be exact, nickname was Pap. My daddy was Dr. Temple, and my name's Hunt. And since I can't stop you from buying my family home out from under me, I don't guess there's any point in trying to keep you off Pap's patio. So, by all means, have a seat." He glared at her to acknowledge the fact she'd already done so.

If she was embarrassed by his bluntness, it didn't show on the fair skin of her face.

Hunt lifted a disposable cup to his lips and took a sip of coffee while he considered the situation that had him over the proverbial barrel. Pap would surely be disgusted if he was aware his grandsons were sitting by calmly while a stranger took possession of the home he'd built with his own two hands. Well, maybe somebody else had done the building, but Pap had drilled the wildcat wells that ultimately paid for Temple Territory, the infamous Kilgore estate gossiped about by everybody who was anybody for the past fifty years. The thirty-eight-room mansion was a legendary landmark, even though it had been vacant since way before Hunt and his brothers were born. The overgrown acres came complete with an oil derrick that served as a monument to the world-renowned East Texas reserve.

Gillian Moore slipped her sunglasses to the top of her head, causing honey-blond bangs to poke up in spikes. She fixed a gaze the color of violet pansies on his cup, and then angled her eyes toward his thermos.

"Is there any chance you have a little more in there?"

"I drink it black and very strong," he warned.

"Me, too."

Hunt set his cup aside, twisted the top off the thermos and filled it nearly to the brim. "What's mine is yours." He offered her the steaming brew. "And as much as I hate to say it, *mi casa es su casa*."

"Excuse me?"

"My home is your home." He jerked his chin toward the Italian renaissance-style structure that had never really been his at all.

She reached over the paper bag on the step between them and accepted the coffee.

"Might as well have these, too." He elbowed the sack, shoving it in her direction.

Shame on you, Hunt. He imagined Alma scolding him. The grandmotherly Mexican woman who'd fed the four Temple boys all their lives would be mortified by his rudeness. She'd kick his ankle with the side of her sneaker and hiss, "How many times have I warned you to check your ego at the bus station? You're a chef, not a heart surgeon. Use the manners you learned from your *madre,* God rest her soul."

Hunt knew better than to argue with Alma, even in his imagination.

Gillian Moore leaned close, unrolled the bag and sniffed the pastries.

"Are these from a local bakery? They smell incredible," she complimented.

"Alma makes fresh sopaipillas every morning."

"Alma?"

"The woman who's been lookin' after my brothers and me since long before our parents died. She's an awesome cook. She might be interested in helping out here when you start hiring your management staff. You'd be lucky to have her," he muttered, imagining his surrogate mother as she wandered about his brother Cullen's quiet kitchen, with so little to do these days.

"Alma knows every nook and cranny of this old place. She brought me here most days during the summers when I was a kid so we could scout the house and outbuildings."

"I hadn't planned on hiring locals for the hotel's management."

Hunt whipped his head toward the comment.

"You can't be serious! Why, that'd be like buying the Alamo and filling it with Russians."

Gillian took a sip from the plastic thermos cap that doubled as a cup. She willed her hand not to shake, determined she wouldn't let nerves caused by Hunt Temple give her plan away.

Only two days ago she'd toured the property with her Realtor. Standing in the windows of what had once been the library, she'd marveled at the potential below. Gillian was sure without a doubt that destiny had led her to this peaceful place to fulfill her dream.

At fifteen her father had gotten her a job working the weekend housekeeping shift at a local Marriott. And even at that young age, she had begun to envision her own boutique hotel. Gillian had no intention of giving her future to a huge corporation and risk being ordered around by some bossy manager who would always want to tell her what to do, just like her father. All these years later, however, thanks to her parents' generosity and faith in her experience and vision, it would only be a matter of a few months before Temple Territory would officially become Moore House.

Gillian raised her eyes to meet the dark gaze of Hunt Temple and couldn't help wondering if he'd ever been mistaken for David Beckham. She'd been warned that the celebrity chef sitting beside her on the steps could be as temperamental in private as he was in the kitchen of a three-star Michelin Guide restaurant. The vein in his throat throbbed as he waited for her response to his insistence that she should hire his friends.

"It's one thing to come in here and snap up a piece of Texas history, but it's another altogether to deny jobs to the local folks," he insisted.

"Allow me to state for the record that I'm hardly *snapping up* this property—it's been on the market since before I was born."

"So, what's the big hurry? My brother says you've insisted on a fast closing and meanwhile I should observe the no-trespassing signs for the first time in my life."

"I presume your brother is McCarthy Temple."

Hunt nodded.

"As a courtesy to your family, my local attorney asked for a few days to notify your brother that the bank has accepted my offer."

Hunt rolled smoky gray eyes skyward and raised his hands in surrender.

"I rest my case," he huffed.

"Meaning?"

"Meaning I don't have any say about all this, it's just secondhand information to me. But at least give me a chance to say goodbye to Pap's place."

"If the estate means so much to you, why haven't you bought it yourself?"

"Honestly?" He lifted his shoulders in a sheepish shrug. "As you said, it's been on the market for decades. I guess I always figured my brothers and I were the only people who might ever want it."

"Well, you figured wrong. I didn't even need to sleep on it overnight before I made my offer. As the old saying goes, 'When you snooze, you lose.'"

"What's your hurry?" Hunt drummed the fingers of his left hand on his knee, impatient for her answer. How ironic that he wanted her to rush her response, just not her actions.

"I have an endless to-do list to get underway and deadlines to meet. Renovations will begin as soon as building permits can be approved."

Hunt folded his arms, the negative body language stretching a snug-fitting T-shirt tighter across the chest and shoulders of a former athlete. His mouth clamped as if pinching in an argument. She hurried on.

"And regarding your comments about hiring locals, I'm sure I'll have opportunities for hourly employees, but I had handpicked my management staff before I ever started researching the right property. They're experienced people I trust, men and women I've worked with over the years who are prepared to relocate."

"Was McCarthy notified about this, as well?"

"There's no reason why he should have been," Gillian countered. "Mr. Temple, people are not fixtures that come with real estate just because they happen to live in the same zip code."

"Will you look around, for cryin' out loud?" He held both arms out, and then turned his head from side to side, giving Gillian a chance to appreciate his handsome profile.

"This place is huge! No matter how much you trust your handpicked buddies, they won't figure out in a year what an old-timer in these parts forgot last week. Alma and her husband, Felix, have had their whole lives to become experts on this place, and they've taught my brothers and me everything there is to know about Temple Territory."

"Moore House." The correction slipped out.

"I beg your pardon?" There was disbelief and an angry edge to the way he asked the question.

She hadn't meant to bring it up in this conversation. But she couldn't unring the bell so she might as well get it over with.

"The name for the estate will be Moore House. And that's just the first of many changes I'll be making. This old place has to be modernized so it will appeal to my guests."

Hunt pushed to his feet. He shoved both hands through his tidy crop of dark hair, and then drew in and expelled several deep breaths as he glowered down at her.

"Since you have so many objections to Temple Territory in its historic condition, what is it that actually appeals to you about this place, Ms. Moore?"

Gillian mirrored his action, stood and stretched her spine, determined to deal with Hunt Temple eyeball to eyeball. She'd done her homework, certain this moment would come. She desperately needed his help, but it would be financially fatal if she tipped her hand or let him intimidate her.

"Mr. Temple, these are tough times, and this is strictly business. If you understood anything about running one, maybe you wouldn't be taking this so personally."

"And by what right do you assume I don't understand how to run a business?"

She smiled, armed and dangerous.

"It's not about assumptions. It's about the facts." She began to recite his résumé.

"You passed up a full ride to the University of Texas on a baseball scholarship to work your way around the U.K. and Europe as a line cook. You eventually earned your cuisine diploma from Le Cordon Bleu in Paris—though it took longer than usual because you struggled with classic French techniques. You shifted continents, became a pretty hot sous-chef in Costa Rica and finally settled into an executive chef position at the Four Seasons in Cancun. But that doesn't appear to have worked out since you're in Kilgore again." She tilted her head. "And unemployed."

The gleam in his eyes said she'd made an impression.

"Did I get the facts straight, Chef?"

"Except for that wisecrack about techniques. I didn't struggle. I just didn't practice. The French preoccupation with peeling vegetables is moot compared to the perfect searing on a tender strip of flank steak."

"I happen to disagree. You can get a hunk of grilled meat on any corner in

Texas, but fine continental cuisine is not so easy to come by around here."

"And that's what you plan to serve in your restaurant, of course." He lowered his eyes, shook his head.

"Of course," she answered, convinced she was absolutely on the right track. "Being unique and a cut above the rest is precisely why our dining experience will be appealing. We'll offer our customers a menu with exquisite choices. In less time than it takes to sing 'The Eyes of Texas,' the private celebrations at Moore House will be the talk of the state."

"Is that a fact?" He was working at being unimpressed.

"It is, indeed. I've employed an extremely high-profile event planner who has guaranteed fabulous bookings and media coverage if Moore House is operative by the holidays."

"Since you have this rush job all figured out, I'm sure this experienced staff of yours includes a classically trained chef, correct?"

Aha! The opportunity she'd hoped for.

She raised her chin and smiled to cover the quivering in her stomach.

I have to appear and sound more confident than I feel. I need this man's help in a big way, and he has no reason to cooperate and every reason to refuse.

She took a deep breath and chose her words carefully.

"No. Not at the moment, anyway. My first choice hasn't worked out, but I'm still hoping he'll reconsider," she lied.

Once Gillian had discovered the connection between the property and culinary celebrity Hunt Temple, she'd realized she was on to something big. Having the TV-acclaimed Cowboy Chef in her kitchen would guarantee the success of her restaurant, even if she could only afford him temporarily.

"Alma's quite an amazing cook, and she's friendly with all the local produce suppliers." Hunt's mouth curved with the suggestion Gillian could sense was coming. "If you should change your opinion about a hunk of grilled meat, I'm sure she'd consider running your kitchen."

Gillian shook her head.

"I have no doubt your friend Alma would make an excellent addition to the kitchen staff. But until my first choice becomes available, I have a substitute in mind. An executive chef with a name and reputation that will draw clients to Moore House like flies to honey. A chef who inherited the ability to do things in a big way. An attractive man who can charm a female diner's eye as well as her palate."

Hunt checked his watch. "So, what time does Jamie Oliver get here?"

Gillian grinned at the idea of the English cooking superstar ordering the staff about in what would soon be her state-of-the-art kitchen.

"I had somebody closer to home in mind." She tipped her head in Hunt's direction.

His gray eyes widened. A shaft of sunshine shot highlights across his hair as the notion lit his brain. He lifted his right hand, touched his index finger to his chest.

"Me?" Hunt's one-word question was incredulous. She couldn't tell whether he was shocked, flattered or offended.

"What do you say, Chef?" Gillian tried to sound self-assured. "How about hanging around Kilgore for a while to help me get Moore House up and running?"

CHAPTER TWO

THE WOMAN STOOD there grinning, obviously pleased with her insulting suggestion. Hunt wondered how on earth she could believe he'd even consider jumping at the bone she'd tossed in the air like a treat for a desperate dog.

Gillian Moore was giving him the opportunity to cook in what should rightfully be his own kitchen, *bless her heart*.

And as second choice, for crying out loud! But even then it was only until the chef she *really* wanted was available.

Hunt's head began to throb as if a plunger had just pushed the Columbian espresso he'd been drinking straight into his brain. He had to shake the caffeine buzz, clear his mind and concentrate. Somehow he had to turn this situation to his advantage, but that wouldn't happen if he reacted by giving words to the bitter taste in his mouth.

When his family had first learned of the sale, his brother Mac had said it was time to accept what was over and done with because they couldn't change it. The facts were that their grandfather's shady deals had cost him fifteen years of freedom in a Texas prison, his wildcatter's fortune, his home and his relationship with his only son, Hunt's father.

Hunt couldn't change the shame that had been left to them as a family legacy, but he could still make a difference in the present and salvage his own name. That is, *if* he kept a cool head, not exactly the strong suit of the men in the Temple family.

Gillian continued to smile, waiting on his answer.

"Well?" She had the nerve to sound perky.

How was it that rich folks seemed to have a knack for morphing somebody else's pain into their gain?

He settled down again on the patio step. She evidently took it as an encouraging sign, because she did the same.

"Say something. What's your gut reaction?" The infernal woman was expecting a positive response.

He held in the rude scoff that threatened to spew. His gut reaction, as she'd put it, was to end this ridiculous conversation, get into his old Jeep and drive away.

And then what?

There was no way to reverse the clock. She'd be the new owner of Temple Territory, no matter how he and his three brothers felt about it. And, as Mac had said, her hotel was better than having the acres leveled for big box stores. And as the eldest brother, Mac had the ultimate say.

Hunt had no choice but to roll with the punches, and that included returning to his hometown, and once again without a place of his own.

"You're always welcome to bunk with me," Cullen had mentioned the night before. "But how long do you reckon you might be hanging around?"

That was an odd question coming from Hunt's identical twin. Weren't they supposed to have some weird compunction to be together? That was the conventional wisdom, but even as boys the two had had little in common. Things were no different today between him and his book-nerd twin. Cullen was perpetually over at the university working on another degree or traveling somewhere to lecture to his fellow history geeks. They wouldn't see much of one another if Hunt stayed with him for a while, so that was a plus. But at thirty-two years old, he couldn't move in with his brother indefinitely.

Gillian tapped the edge of her cup with the tip of one short nail, reminding him she expected a response. She was a decisive woman who'd made a multimillion-dollar purchase after a few hours of consideration. He was nothing more than a speed bump in the parking lot of her plans. He had to make up his mind before she moved on to a third choice. There were excellent chefs in Dallas and Houston who would jump at the chance to get out of the city.

Hunt leaned forward, an elbow on each knee, one hand gripping the other to brace himself for the counterproposal he was about to offer.

"I hate to fly. I'd rather have a root canal. Once during a flight from Greece to Costa Rica, I got vertigo. Those were the longest and most miserable hours of my life." Hunt closed his eyes for a moment against the recollection. "There was nothing I could do but let the world spin around me while the plane thumped through one pocket of turbulence after another. Once the aircraft landed in San José, I still had to suffer a wild ride with a Nigerian taxi driver to the nearest *clinica*. When I finally got enough medication in me to calm the vertigo, I prayed I'd never be in such a vulnerable position again."

Gillian listened with her sandy blond brows pulled together in concern, a "what's your point?" question in her all-business eyes and a not-so-surreptitious glance at her wristwatch.

"I know." He bobbed his head in respect for her busy schedule. "But I told you that story so I could tell you this story. When I sat down with my three brothers yesterday morning, and McCarthy gave us the news that Temple Territory had been purchased, it was like being on that awful flight. For the past twenty-four hours, the world has been spinning out of control." Hunt smiled. He needed to appear and sound sincere. "I guess, in a way, you've given me some hope, and for that I should be grateful."

Her shoulders relaxed and a glimmer of relief appeared on the face that he had to admit was Katherine Heigl beautiful.

"So, you'll accept my offer?"

There was cautious expectation in her voice. Maybe she didn't have a third option up her sleeve after all.

"It's more complicated than that." He squinted and pressed his molars together, trying to seem stressed, as if he had a big decision to make. "You're not the only person who's aware I've left the Four Seasons. I have several other opportunities on the table already, so staying here even temporarily could cost me a much bigger deal."

It might have been true. There was no offer at the moment, but his agent was working on it. He'd had a steady stream of offers since winning a reality cooking show that had given him the nickname "the

Cowboy Chef." Something would come along soon. Sadly, that something would likely take him far away from his hometown. And this is where he needed to be, if he was ever to become as close to his brothers as he'd once been.

"I'll make it worth your while financially."

He held a palm outward and shook his head.

"If I hang around, it won't be because of the money, it'll be for my family's sake. Dad would want one of his sons to keep an eye on what you're doin' with Pap's place."

Gillian crossed her arms, and lowered her pointed chin a bit, causing long strands of blond hair to fall across her shoulders. "You do understand you'd have no vote in my plans, correct?"

"I didn't ask for a vote, just a voice. An astute businesswoman should be open-minded, willing to listen to another opinion."

She nodded, seemed to accept his logic. "So, do we have an agreement?"

"Not yet. I do have one condition, and it's a deal breaker."

"Let me guess. You want an offer in writing."

"Yeah, but I want the offer in writing to Alma and Felix. You make them part of your staff for as long as you own the property, and I'll stick around for a while. Between the three of us, we can teach you the history of our neck of the woods."

FINALLY. THE MAN got to the bottom line.

Fair enough. Gillian appreciated a rousing negotiation and admired his family loyalty. She'd benefit from Hunt's ability to help her design a state-of-the-art kitchen, then cook fabulous food and charm her well-heeled patrons with his Cowboy Chef persona for as long as she could afford him. But she wasn't sure she wanted to hear the man's opinions, and she definitely hadn't asked for his historical mentoring.

"As I've mentioned, I do my homework, and I'm pretty confident that I'm up to speed on Texas history." She lifted her cup and took another sip.

"Is that a fact? So you've heard all about the monster sea snake that lives in Lake Cherokee, have you?"

Gillian sloshed a few drops from her cup. The dark brew splashed on her scarlet bag, a treasure from her favorite resale shop in Old Town Alexandria.

"And you're aware that this very parcel of land was farmed for hundreds of years by members of the Caddo Nation?" He pointed toward the ground beneath their feet. "What's left of the Caddo tribe regularly tries to lay claim to Temple Territory, pointing to the well their ancestors dug as proof of their rights. Pap built the mansion around the well out of respect for the spirits they believe still abide here."

She shook her head, wondering if she should speak to her lawyer concerning this nonsense about that nasty old well in the courtyard.

"And, of course, you've heard Temple Territory is cursed, right? In all these years, no honest business would touch it because my Pap was branded as a thief who made his fortune stealing a few hundred million barrels from a major oil company."

"No, I wasn't aware of any of that," she admitted. This was all fresh news.

It was true she'd been reading about East Texas in general but hadn't yet found the hours to dig into local folklore. He was right. She could definitely use area experts and storytellers who'd share the fantasies as well as the facts of the place. Like Hunt himself, some of it could become part of the new ambience she'd use to entice and entertain the guests at Moore House.

Gillian pulled a tissue from inside her bag and swiped at the drizzling droplets of coffee atop it while she considered the appeal of Alma's homemade pastries, made fresh each day. A smart hotelier offered her guests an experience they could not have elsewhere. What was the use in having the Cowboy Chef in her kitchen even short-term if she didn't have the tall Texas tales to go along with him?

"Say something. What's your gut reaction?" Hunt mocked her earlier question.

She shifted her attention from the coffee

stain on her favorite purse to the alluring face of the youngest Temple brother. She'd never considered she could attract the reality television celebrity, but that was before her real estate agent had insisted Gillian get on the next flight for a visit to Temple Territory. Finding the perfect property that just happened to be connected to Hunt Temple couldn't be interpreted as anything other than providence.

Gillian recognized her equal in the man beside her. He'd turned a problem to his advantage, just as she'd have done. Another item on the list of critical information she'd keep to herself.

Hunt still had the body of an athlete, was slap-your-sister hot and possessed a cache of local secrets. He was well traveled in spite of his fear of flying, and probably spoke a few phrases in several languages. So she steamrolled ahead with her plan, just as her father would do in her shoes.

"My gut tells me to meet your condition—if you promise to stay for as long as I require your help." That would help her rush a grand opening during the holiday

season and establish her no-nonsense reputation. Maybe she'd even convince him to
stick around longer. Or not.

"I'll have the agreement drawn up by
my lawyer, and he'll be in touch with you
later today."

She offered her hand to make it official.
"Deal?"

He took her fingers gently in his, raised
them to his face and kissed the backside
of them lightly.

"Deal," he murmured.

A shiver ran from her knuckles to the
pleasure center of her brain. She gave a
nod to acknowledge the gesture, and then
slipped her hand away from his touch.

Needing a distraction from the warmth
of his lips still on her flesh, she glanced
down at the paper sack and then reached
in for a homemade sopaipilla.

The crispy pastry melted on her tongue,
leaving a hint of honey and earthy sweet-
ness.

"Have you had breakfast?"

"No," she mumbled, savoring another bite.

"My brother Cullen's place is only a couple miles from here. If Alma's there, she'll be happy to whip up some killer huevos rancheros. Her tortillas are always made from scratch." His eyes sparked at the mention of the Mexican favorites.

"Maybe another morning. Today I'm in the mood for something French prepared by my new executive chef."

"Does an omelet *au fromage* appeal to you?"

"Does Limburger cheese stink?"

"Well, then, let's go." Without hesitation he stood and offered his hand to help her to her feet, then swept his palm toward the side drive where both their vehicles were parked. She stepped toward her rental car with his footsteps a respectful distance behind.

"I'll follow you in my car."

He was being suspiciously agreeable. Over the course of their brief negotiation, the man had morphed from righteous indignation to effusive gratitude. Somewhere in that pendulum swing of emotion was the real Hunt Temple, and given long enough she might be able to sift through the chaff and find the grain. If not, that was okay, too.

She'd come to Texas to realize her dream, not analyze a man.

A SHORT WHILE LATER, Gillian stepped across the threshold of Cullen's home and followed his lead straight to the kitchen. The hacienda-style room was cozy and welcoming. Hunt pulled a tall hand-tooled stool away from the mosaic-tile counter and held the chair while she stepped up onto it and settled in to watch him work. He took a knee-length white apron from a drawer and secured it around his waist. Then he reached for a skillet, sprinkled it with oil and positioned it on a lit burner.

He grabbed two eggs from the fridge and cracked them against the side of a clear mixing bowl. A shard of white shell fell atop the golden yellow yolks.

"Glad I've already got the job," he said as he fished out the fragment.

"Am I making you nervous?"

"In a way," he admitted, above the fury

of his whisk. "It's a bit unusual to be hired before you ever serve a meal to the boss."

"Oh, you've served me before."

Hunt turned puzzled eyes her way, the brows above his slate-colored irises raised in question.

"I was checking out the small hotels in Cancun last summer. I had the opportunity to eat in your restaurant on an evening when you were expediting the kitchen."

"And how was your meal?" He was fishing for a compliment.

"The snapper was overcooked and underseasoned. I sent it back to the kitchen."

The ultimate insult hit the chef like a dart to his chest. Hunt melodramatically clutched his heart with both palms and mock-swooned against the kitchen wall, and Gillian could swear her own heart reacted, as well.

Being around this man was either going to be great fun or a great big mistake.

CHAPTER THREE

"DON'T HOLD BACK, little brother. Tell us how you *really* feel about your rich boss lady." Joiner, the middle Temple brother, poked fun at Hunt's diatribe over his new employer.

"I can't help it. The more I listen to her big ideas, the more they worry me." Hunt sank deeper into the sofa in McCarthy's office. McCarthy sat behind the desk, and Joiner sprawled on the sofa beside Hunt. Cullen was in a corner, his nose in a book. "She's determined to import a bunch of strangers so they can create a new 'culture.'" He made quote marks in the air. "This is Texas, for pity's sake. Why would anybody in their right mind want to replace the historical culture of Temple Territory that already exists? She's on a collision course with reality, and I'm afraid my reputation as a chef could go down in flames with her."

"Oh, get over yourself, *Cowboy Chef*," Joiner said, making fun of Hunt's television identity. A lifelong lover of horses, Joiner was the closest thing to a real cowboy in the family. He'd always held it over the heads of his younger brothers, whom he'd berated as a bookworm and a kitchen mouse, regardless of the fact that both could have played professional baseball.

"Life will continue," Joiner insisted. "You have to move on to another dream now that McCarthy's let the estate get away from you."

"Just wait a doggone minute." McCarthy's dark stare landed on each of his brothers. "I'm fed up with you three holding me accountable for seeing Daddy's mission to clear our name accomplished. We've all wasted a lot of years talking a good game, but none of us ever put our shoulder to the wheel and made things happen. You can't blame me because the bank finally found a buyer, and reclaiming Pap's place is never gonna happen."

Cullen took a break from the textbook he was thumbing through. "I'm not so sure Daddy would want a lot of attention drawn to the Temple name now anyway, not after all the years it took for the gossip to die down. Why, wasn't he in agreement with Pap's decision not to come home after he got out of prison?"

"Yes, but he never dreamed he wouldn't see Pap again," McCarthy said.

"It's the old man's fault for going out to West Texas and getting himself killed working on that dangerous gas well. Otherwise we might have grown up with the flesh-and-blood Pap instead of this infamous legend Daddy spent his adult life trying to live down," Cullen insisted.

McCarthy sighed and dropped his chin to his chest. He pushed out of his chair and moved to the foot of the desk.

"Pay attention while I spell this out for you knuckleheads one last time." McCarthy slapped the tabletop to draw Joiner's gaze away from his iPhone. "I was only a senior in high school when we had the conversation, but Daddy was clear on this subject, almost as if he sensed he wouldn't be around to do it himself. Pap stayed away so Daddy and Mama wouldn't have to raise us in earshot of constantly wagging tongues. Daddy was establishing himself at the hospital when Pap was paroled. Coming home would only have stirred the pot again. So he left well enough alone, and on the day he walked free, Pap went in the opposite direction."

"So he pretty much abandoned Daddy."

"Cullen, it's not as if he was left on a doorstep in a basket. He was a grown man with four boys of his own. Pap did what he thought was right, and Daddy let him go. It was years before Daddy was finally able to put behind him the stigma that went along with Pap's crime, and by then the old man was long dead. Still, Daddy felt he needed to forgive his father, and do something public to restore honor to our name."

"Why didn't Daddy just buy Temple Territory himself?"

"Like everybody else in Texas, he believed the place was jinxed, purchased and cursed by hot oil. But once he found out

Pap had been killed, Daddy fixed his mind on going out to that well site to mark his father's grave properly."

"And they didn't make it," Cullen said quietly.

The private aircraft had gone down in the Apache Mountains, killing the two on board and leaving four teenage boys in Kilgore in the care of Alma and Felix Ortiz.

They all fell silent, and Hunt decided to change the mood of the room.

"Well, I never bought into that business about the property being cursed, and with any luck Pap's place isn't completely out of my reach yet," Hunt announced.

Three pairs of expectant eyes waited for him to continue.

"How's that?" McCarthy spoke up as he settled again into his chair.

"In case nobody's been listening, I've got a job—at *Moore House*. I'm on the inside, and I plan to stay all up in that lady's business to slow her down before she changes anything that can't be put right."

"Instead of fighting the inevitable, why

don't you tell some of those wealthy friends
you've been feedin' for free all these years
that it's payback time," Joiner snapped.
"Get them to invest in your own restaurant.
You can call it Hunt's Hangout or something equally sophisticated."

"You have no idea how much capital that
would require." Hunt had already done the
math for himself out of morbid curiosity
and been depressed for days by the number.

"But I'm sure Gillian Moore does, and
she didn't seem to have any problem round-
ing up the cash. So instead of whining, why
don't you put on your big-boy boots and
compete with her?" Cullen chucked a wad
of paper at his twin.

It bounced off the center of Hunt's forehead. He rubbed the spot where a pointy
corner had poked his flesh. Instead of ad-
monishing his brother for almost putting
his eye out, Hunt marked the moment. He
went all in. He'd always planned to have
his own place one day. If somebody was
going to change the fate of Temple Territory, why shouldn't it be a Temple heir?
And once Gillian Moore realized she'd

bitten off more than she could chew, she might be willing to take a loss for the property and go home, leaving Pap's place to its rightful owners. And leaving Hunt to repair the damage the made-for-TV Cowboy Chef had done to his real-life relationships in Kilgore.

"THESE RIDICULOUS DOORS have to come down," Gillian instructed a prospective contractor as they went room by room through the mansion several days later. For the past two hours she'd itemized the work that would give the interior of the house a crucial face-lift. The Italian renaissance exterior and tile roof were still in amazingly fine shape. But inside the fifty-year-old home, it was dark and cavernous, in desperate need of modern lighting and plumbing, just for starters.

"Yes, get rid of these first thing," she repeated.

"You can't be serious." Hunt's voice echoed in the dining room. Obviously he'd returned sooner than Gillian had expected. The man who'd be an asset once they opened was becoming a pebble in her pump during the renovations, prying into every detail of her plan.

She tucked her small notebook into her shoulder bag, gave a nod of apology to the contractor and turned to address Hunt. "Of course I'm serious. I can't have Wild West saloon doors in the entrance to a European-themed restaurant."

"Do you at least plan to recycle the doors and use them someplace else?"

She flicked one of the heavy panels. It creaked to and fro on rusty hinges. "I plan to make these sad old things the first layer of the bonfire."

Hunt's jaws clenched, as they had frequently in the past several days. Color shot from his collarbone to his hairline. As was the case with many a temperamental chef, the man took himself way too seriously.

"May I speak with you privately, please?" Keeping his voice low seemed to take effort.

Gillian followed his lead as he crossed the soon-to-be-expanded dining room floor and headed for the front foyer. When they were a safe distance from anyone who might repeat their conversation, he spun to face her.

"This is the first of what I hope will be many teachable moments." The mercurial man seemed to struggle for self-control.

Gillian's schedule was tight. She had back-to-back interviews with contractors. She wanted to dismiss this interruption by Hunt, but she *had* agreed to at least listen to his objections.

"So what's the big deal about those slabs of wood?"

"Those *slabs of wood* are ax-hewn heart of loblolly pine. Antiques dealers scour the countryside for such quality reclaimed lumber."

"Okay, so they're worth a few bucks. We'll put them in the yard-sale pile instead." She turned away. Hunt caught her by the wrist, but let go as soon as her eyes met his again.

"The historic value is greater than the price of the wood. Those boards came from Temple Number One, the first wildcat well Pap brought in. He pried the pine from the drilling rig floor. Built and hung those swinging doors himself."

"Well, then, he should have been convicted on an extra count for his bad taste." Gillian knew instantly that her sorry excuse for a joke was a mistake. But instead of the angry response she deserved and expected, Hunt got quiet and moved to stare out the cracked bay window.

The roots of Gillian's hair flushed hot, a sure sign a woman in the Moore family was embarrassed. Any moment she'd break into a sweat and her cheeks would glow as brightly as taillights in morning traffic.

"I'm sorry, Hunt." She wanted for all the world to dig a hole and crawl into it. "What I said was cruel and I apologize."

"What you said was fairly accurate." He faced her, a hint of a smile curving his full lips. "Alma always said that Pap's interior design left a lot to be desired. But he did things his own way."

Hunt tipped his head up. His gaze scanned the dark walls and shadowy high ceilings of the foyer. "No matter what people said about him in the end, our daddy told us Pap had guts in spades—and an ornery nature any mule would envy."

"The family resemblance is strong," she cautiously teased. Hunt had kindly let her off when she deserved a boot in the behind for her snide comment.

The cell phone in her pocket buzzed. She checked the caller ID.

Dang it, Father, what is it now?

She sent him directly to voice mail, making a mental note to get to his message before her next appointment. Her father was driving her nuts, questioning and second-guessing her every decision. At least he was over a thousand miles away. Having her controlling father any closer would have made this project impossible.

"So how about a stay of execution for the doors?"

For a split second Gillian was tempted to give in to Hunt's hopeful voice and appealing eyes just to make him go away and let her return to work. But the moment passed. She'd do things her way, and neither Hunt Temple nor James Moore would tell her what to do. Still, there was a story behind the pieces that added ambience, albeit in the wrong place.

She offered a compromise. "We can use them in the spa. We'll work the doors into the decor of the juice bar."

"Spa? You haven't mentioned a spa." Hunt's brows scrunched in concern.

"Phase II," she explained. And that was all the explanation he'd get on her future plans. She could just imagine his objections when he found out that smelly Caddo well would be filled in and covered over with a tile floor when she enclosed the courtyard. She'd keep that to herself until he needed to know, if ever.

Hunt squinted in thought, as if he was considering her alternative suggestion for the doors. Not that she could let his opinions matter too much in the end. Gillian would only get one grab at the brass ring. She hadn't put her reputation and her parents' retirement fund on the line to have her plans questioned by a professional foodie.

Even if the foodie was the talented, unpredictable and quite handsome Cowboy Chef.

CHAPTER FOUR

"I HAVE A better idea for the doors." Hunt tilted his head and motioned with his hand for Gillian to follow him. He smiled at the tapping of her heels behind him. He was making progress with the boss lady already.

"Hunt, I'm too busy for this right now."

Maybe not so much progress after all.

He continued toward the old kitchen.

"You're not listening to me," she insisted, but remained close behind. "I'm booked solid this afternoon, and I have to return that call. Your granddaddy's rustic old doors have been collecting dust for decades. There's no reason to get in a dither about them right this minute."

"All evidence to the contrary since you were about to put a piece of Texas history on the scrap pile. I'd say a dither is exactly what's called for, and you might agree in about thirty seconds."

He crossed the scuffed terra-cotta tiles that led to the large walk-in pantry. Once inside, he reached up to tug a length of kitchen twine dangling from overhead, weighted decades ago by a lead swivel sinker from somebody's tackle box. A single bulb lit the space dimly, but the light was sufficient to make Hunt's point. The roomy closet was lined with thick slabs of knotty pine, the golden color deepened with age to the hue of maple syrup.

Gillian stepped forward, ran her palm across the smooth wall, her face giving away her appreciation of the reclaimed timbers.

"I hadn't given this closet any attention. Is this the same wood?"

Hunt nodded. "When the drilling derrick at Temple One was torn down to make room for a mechanical horse-head pump, Pap hauled the lumber here to be used in the construction of his home."

"So, Mason Dixon Temple was a conservationist before conservation was cool."

"I guess that's as good a way to put it as any. How about if we hang those doors here? I presume you plan to offer an in-kitchen dining experience, and this pantry could be a focal point with an interesting story."

"To be honest, I hadn't considered the idea of special seating in the kitchen but I understand it's become quite popular. If we include that in the plan, won't the diners be in your way?"

"We'll have plenty of additional space once that far wall is blown out to accommodate the walk-in cooler." He pointed toward the row of windows she'd marked for demolition to expand the footprint. "We'll put seating for eight along the south wall, and the pine pantry will be storage for our selection of fine wines. A dinner party in our kitchen will be on every hostess's wish list for the New Year."

The nod of her head was nearly imperceptible, but it was enough. He'd scored a point. She stepped into the open space he'd envisioned for the prep stations and cooking surfaces.

"Have you given any thought to the layout of the countertops and appliances?"

It took every shred of manners his mama taught him to hold back the rude response that rushed to his lips. Gillian Moore wasn't stupid, and he was pretty sure she wasn't downright mean. He could only surmise it hadn't crossed the woman's mind that he'd wandered the halls of Temple Territory for countless hours, dreaming and planning of what he'd do with the place. But he'd never imagined it would all be for somebody else.

"I've laid out this kitchen nine ways from Friday and I've planned out exactly how it should operate. I've been remodeling it in my mind since I was sixteen and fried my first green tomato."

"Then why didn't you make it happen yourself?" There was annoyance in the way she barked the question.

"I never imagined anybody would make the investment in this place, given its reputation." Hearing his excuse made Hunt feel like the whiner his brothers had accused him of being that very same morning.

"Well, you were wrong. It only took me

one walk-through to realize this property could be spectacular."

"So you've already told me." He scuffed his hand through his hair, Gillian's aggravation spilling over to him. "Just give me the budget and I'll get the best return for your investment."

She retrieved a notepad from her purse, flipped over a few pages and then held it up so Hunt could read the bottom-line figure, circled in red ink. "We must stay within that amount."

Hunt exhaled a soft whistle. He'd be bitter about her ability to exercise such generosity if he wasn't going to enjoy spending the rich girl's money.

"Well, can you make it work?"

"I'll see what I can do." He feigned uncertainty. "There's wiggle room, of course."

"None whatsoever." She flipped her notepad closed and poked it into her bag. "I don't intend to rob Peter to pay Paul during this project. I've worked this budget out with my financial advisor *nine ways from Friday,* as you so eloquently put it. There's no reason we can't open Moore House on schedule and without breaking the bank."

Moore House. Cold chills rippled up Hunt's spine each time he heard the name. Surely the sensation was caused by Pap rolling over in his unmarked grave.

MOORE HOUSE. JUST the mention of it comforted Gillian like a thick quilt on a bleak winter day. Her parents' investment of their years of vigilant saving simply had to bear fruit, and in a big way. There could be no other outcome, or her folks would be working the rest of their lives, and she'd never hear the end of it from her father.

Gillian loved the hospitality business and would work in corporate service if there was no other choice. But caring for her own guests under her own roof was her dream.

She'd been short with Hunt just now about his ambitions, but the man had dragged his feet and let a golden opportunity pass him by. That was his issue. She had plenty of her own.

Highest on the list was to meet her grand opening deadline to make the most of the holiday season. To do it, she'd personally have to watch every penny, and that meant keeping a close eye on Hunt. Everything he put on his inventory list had to be absolutely necessary and the best value possible. She'd drive a rental truck to Dallas and pick up the stainless-steel appliances herself if it would save a buck.

"You're the boss," Hunt reminded Gillian, returning her attention to their discussion. "Far be it from me to argue if you want to cut corners."

"You can't be serious." His crooked smirk revealed that the man was intentionally goading her. "That's a very generous budget. If you're not able to handle the job, I'm sure I can find a capable chef, even if I have to take a risk on an unknown," she bluffed.

"Don't get your knickers in a twist. We made a deal, and I intend to keep my end of the bargain."

Her cell buzzed again. Gillian slipped her hand inside the pocket of her shoulder bag, retrieved the phone and, no surprise, noted her father had called twice in the past fifteen minutes.

"My knickers are none of your concern. But our contract certainly is, so speak now or be legally bound through the end of the year."

He held his palms outward. "I apologize, that comment was inappropriate. How can I make it up to you?"

The phone sounded once more. She held up her index finger to indicate she needed a minute to take the call. With the phone to her ear, she turned away, briefly but firmly telling her father she would call him shortly. Then she faced Hunt again, the enormity of the undertaking hitting her. Maybe she could delegate.

"Since you offered, would you meet with the kitchen designer for me? He's on his way, and I still have a lot to cover with the contractor in the other room who's probably charging me by the hour for this meeting. So I've got to go. Can I trust you to handle things with the designer and report to me as soon as your meeting is finished?"

"Of course. How about if I give you a full rundown over dinner tonight?"

"Dinner?" She wasn't sure it was wise to spend an hour with Hunt away from the workplace. Tongues would wag in this small Texas town. "Where?"

"My brother's house, unless you'd rather go out."

"Actually, a home-cooked meal sounds wonderful."

It had only been a week, but Gillian was already tired of the small restaurant in the chain hotel where she was staying.

"Any special requests?" Hunt asked.

"I'm game for something local, whatever's in season."

"Right now, squirrel is in season." He clamped his lips together to suppress a grin.

She slanted her eyes at some invisible point above him and considered how to respond.

"Surprise me," she finally challenged.

"Consider it done. Now go take care of your remodeling man, and I'll deal with the kitchen guy. What's his name, by the way?"

She checked her notes. "Steve Froehlich."

"Froehlich? I don't know of any Froehlichs in these parts."

"He's from Houston. Since he's working another job in Tyler at the moment, he agreed to drive over."

"Did you invite anybody local to bid? I'm sure I could make a good recommendation if you'll give me a day to ask around." He snapped his fingers. "I played ball with a guy named Karl Gates who works with his dad. They're the best carpenters in Rusk County. What do you say I give him a call?"

She raised a palm against his offer. "Don't start with that good-old-boy network business. I'm aware of how you guys operate."

"I haven't done anything to deserve your suspicion." Hunt took offense.

"You haven't done anything *yet*." Gillian motioned with two fingers from her eyes to Hunt's, then turned and hurried away.

The clock was ticking and she was spending her parents' money.

But in her rush to get things done, had she put too much trust in Hunt too soon?

THE MAN WHO answered the front door of the home that evening was the mirror image of Hunt, but Gillian realized instantly it was his twin. Hunt's dark brown hair was neatly cropped; his face always clean-shaven.

This man's hair was on the shaggy side with a couple days' worth of very appealing stubble on his chin. And in contrast to Hunt's *GQ* style, this twin was dressed comfortably in a flannel shirt and jeans faded by years of wear.

"Gillian Moore?" he asked. When she smiled, he offered his hand and drew her across the threshold. "I'm Hunt's older and better-lookin' twin brother, Cullen."

"Go ahead and admit that you're also smarter than the rest of us," Hunt called from inside the house. "You'll reveal your brilliance eventually, you always do, so get it over with up front."

"He's right," Cullen agreed, lowering his chin modestly. "I am the best-educated of the Temple brothers, but I'm not so sure that makes me smarter than anybody besides Hunt, which ain't sayin' much."

"Whoa, I always heard twins were kindred souls, each protective of the other."

"Yeah, that's what the experts say, but if Hunt didn't resemble me quite so much, I'd figure our folks had brought home the wrong kid."

Gillian followed Cullen across the herringbone entryway and into a family room. The floor-to-ceiling shelves on three walls were so tightly packed with hardbound volumes that the space resembled a library in need of organization. An oversize sofa and chairs occupied the center of the room that was strewn with newspapers. A large partner's desk laden with a desktop computer, a laptop and many more books crowded one corner. As she took in the homey clutter, she knew this was definitely not the meticulous lifestyle of her executive chef.

Hunt emerged from behind the kitchen bar where he'd served her breakfast a few days earlier. An apron covered his clothing from the waist down, but the stark white seemed to accentuate the fit of his red polo shirt and the definition in his arms. The man was a feast for the eyes.

"I'd apologize for my brother's cluttered home if it would make him change, but this mess is part of who he is. His quirky personality just happens to have tipped over and spilled everywhere."

Hunt's gaze swept the room, followed by a disbelieving shake of his head.

"While our mama was alive, she made Cullen keep the books in his bedroom. But once we lost our parents, all restraints were off. And instead of growing out of his obsession for academia, this big galoot and his size-twelve feet grew into it."

Gillian stepped close to one shelf and stared in awe at the private collection, many of which were textbooks.

"If you must have a touch of OCD," Gillian said, "I agree that the printed word is a great obsession to choose. And if you've read each of these, you must be very smart, indeed, Cullen."

"Thank you, ma'am. Hunt said that you were sharp as a new pickax and pretty as a baby goat, but he didn't mention you're a good judge of character, too."

"Uh-huh." Hunt cleared his throat, making the point that the conversation had gone on long enough.

"Yes, little bro. I remember the instructions you gave me. Let the pretty woman into the house and then make myself scarce."

Cullen glanced at Gillian and raised his gaze to the rafters overhead. "This is the thanks I get for taking in my sibling and letting him have the run of my kitchen."

"If you expect to share in this meal, you'll get out while the gettin' is still good, or I'll put you to work."

"I sure hope you're partial to squirrel, Miss Moore," Cullen said with a grin before ambling down the long hallway and turning out of sight.

CHAPTER FIVE

"SQUIRREL?" GILLIAN SQUEAKED the question and Hunt smiled inwardly.

"Yep, and you're in luck. These two tree-dwelling rodents were flying through the pines just this morning. Felix was honored to donate them for our dinner."

He saw her swallow.

"Well, I did leave the menu up to you, and whatever it is you're preparing smells divine," she said.

"That's nice to hear. Some say people eat with their eyes first, but I believe the aroma sets the mood for the meal. May I start you off this evening with a drop of the grape?"

He stooped to open a wine cabinet and pulled out two uncorked bottles. "When Cullen was working on one of his degrees, French history maybe, he became a wine aficionado. I gotta admit he keeps a pretty nice selection in the house."

Hunt angled the bottles for her to inspect the labels. Her violet eyes widened with recognition.

"I'd love to sample the Rothschild Bordeaux, but I'm driving, and I have a lot more work to do tonight, so I hope you'll give me a rain check. Some sparkling water will be fine, if you have it."

"That we do."

He returned the wine bottles to the rack and busied himself dropping ice into two chilled glasses before filling both with Perrier. He set Gillian's glass on a cocktail napkin and motioned for her to have a seat at the tall counter tiled with a hacienda-style colorful mosaic.

"Pardon my backside, but I should see how the braising is coming along." He lifted the lid off a deep cast-iron skillet and poked at the contents inside with a long-handled fork. "Tell me about the rest of your day."

"You first," she countered. "How did things go with Mr. Froehlich?"

Hunt replaced the lid on the skillet and transferred the pan to a hot oven, choosing his words carefully. "I'm not convinced your fellow from Houston is the right man for this job."

"Now, why was that exactly what I expected to hear from you?"

"I beg your pardon." He gave her a wide-eyed glare for a moment, then reached for the panko bread crumbs. He upended the box into a mixing bowl.

"Cut the innocent act, Hunt. Did you even review his drawings?"

"I certainly did, but Froehlich doesn't share our vision for retaining the integrity of Pap's original design."

She slapped her palm on the tile countertop.

"Listen to me! There is no such thing as *our vision*. I can't afford to pacify your need to maintain some emotional connection to a place that was your grandfather's half a century ago."

Her words stung. Not because she was right, but because she was giving Hunt credit he didn't deserve.

If he truly felt a deep-seated yearning to bridge the family connection to Temple Territory, wouldn't he have made it happen long before now? Wasn't all his talk at this point more selfish than selfless?

Man, he hated moments of revelation. It was why he avoided psychotherapy like a swarm of mosquitos.

So now what? Let the boss lady continue to believe he might be altruistic, or admit he'd only been pursuing his own aspirations? He wasn't ready to tip his hand quite yet.

"You're right." He reached into the fridge for the colander of zucchini, keeping his eyes averted so she couldn't read the lie he was about to voice.

"This isn't about me and my warped sense of family pride. My obligation is to you and to doing everything in my power to help you meet your deadlines."

She was quiet while he busied himself slicing the dark green squash and tossing uniform discs into the bread crumbs.

"Cat got your tongue?" He glanced up from the cutting board.

"For a moment, yes." She took a sip from her glass. "I seem to be criticizing you a lot. That's not fair or normally my nature to be so judgmental. But I'm out of my element right now, and I'm determined to keep a laser focus on the prize."

Hunt set a small bowl of spiced pecan halves on the ledge before Gillian. "Alma says these are good for the digestion."

"Am I going to require digestive help after this meal?" She scooped up several pecans and popped them into her mouth.

He took one of the homemade treats as well and savored Alma's special combination of cinnamon and cloves.

"Only if you eat too much squirrel," he warned. "So, what is your element? You can tell mine is a kitchen. How would you describe your comfort zone?"

"That's a question without an easy answer." She reached for more pecans.

"And that's a stall tactic."

"Not this time." As she shook her head, the blunt tips of silky blond hair brushed her shoulders. "I love everything about the boutique hotel business. The buzz of a reservation line. The hush of a linen closet. The madness of a busy front desk. The clink of silver on china in the dining room."

"The *cha-ching* of the cash register," he interjected.

"That, too," she laughed.

He enjoyed the sound of her laughter, so relaxed and different from the way she barked orders.

"The point is that I'm more at home in a hotel than I've ever been in our family's house. Now I'll have both under one roof."

"So you plan to live there?" He hadn't considered the possibility.

"Oh, certainly. I can just imagine the luxury of coffee on that back terrace every morning."

He raised his brows. "Can you now?"

She dipped her chin in apology.

His guest seemed to keep forgetting he'd had many years to consider what life at the landmark mansion had to offer.

He tossed the mixing bowl to coat each slice of zucchini with bread crumbs and then eased the silver-dollar-sized pieces into hot canola oil where they would fry up crispy and light.

"Can I do anything to help?" she offered.

"You can set the table, if you don't mind. Cullen keeps his dishes and flatware in that hutch against the wall." He motioned with a slotted metal spoon, and then stooped to check the flame beneath his frying pan. "I hope it won't offend you to eat in the kitchen. There's a perfectly good dining room across the hall, but my doofus brother uses it to store his research files instead of for the purpose God intended."

Cullen appeared, relaxed and lazy, as always. How he'd managed to get four degrees without breaking a sweat was a mystery to Hunt, who stressed over every element on a plate.

"Are you talkin' about me again, little bro?"

"Guilty as charged. How about giving Gillian a hand? And if you own a cloth napkin, could you show her where you hide them?"

Cullen reached over Gillian's head to retrieve colorful Fiestaware plates from the top shelf. "I only own a couple, and they're in the hall bathroom."

Gillian's eyes gleamed with humor as they met Hunt's.

"Is there any point in asking why?"

"I should do laundry soon. All the company hand towels are in the hamper, and the napkins fit that little short bar in there."

"Il n'est pas juste," Hunt muttered.

"I could write a book on Louis XIV, but I don't speak a word of French, and Hunt knows it," Cullen complained to Gillian.

"He said you're not right."

"Oh, he says that regularly." Cullen waived away his twin's comment and carried the dishes to the pedestal table that had come from their childhood kitchen. "Hey, where'd you find this?" Cullen ran his fingers over the white cloth that was draped across the scarred family heirloom.

"In one of Mama's trunks." Rummaging through the linens Alma had saved for him was always bittersweet. It was still surprising that he missed his folks so much after all these years. "Thanks for letting me store her things here until I have a permanent place of my own."

"Hey, what are big brothers for?"

"That's a question I ask myself frequently."

GILLIAN LISTENED TO the banter between the men and wondered what it must have been like with a house full of siblings. Being an only child was lonely. Probably another reason she enjoyed the hotel business so much. There was always someone to talk with, someone to learn from, someone to help out.

This good-natured rivalry was so different. Nice. Evidence that Hunt had been reared by people who loved him and in a town where he felt at home. No wonder he'd found it hard to settle down in another city, much less another country.

"Gillian, would you please do the honors?" Hunt handed her the open bottle of Perrier and gestured toward the fresh stemware on the table Cullen was clumsily preparing. As she moved to each place setting to fill the goblet, she rearranged the cutlery and positioned the plates just so.

Hunt rewarded her surreptitious efforts with a smile that showed even white teeth. His appeal struck her with a fresh punch each time he caught her eye. No wonder he'd been such a hit on reality TV.

The heat of attraction crept up her neck. To cover her discomfort, Gillian dropped into a chair and took a sip from the glass she'd just poured.

"Hunt, our guest has claimed her spot at the table, so can we sit down and eat now?"

"By all means." Hunt motioned for Cullen to take a seat, and then put serving bowls and a woven basket on the table. With care he placed a thick trivet in the center to protect his mother's cloth, and then transferred the heavy iron skillet from the oven to the table. He whisked away the lid to reveal the steaming, mouthwatering contents.

"What do you think, Gilly? Do you mind if I call you Gilly?" Cullen asked what seemed to be a rhetorical question. "That's a Texas-sized squirrel if I've ever encountered one."

She leaned toward the skillet and peered at the bubbling cream sauce and mystery meat that was not so mysterious after all.

"That's not a squirrel." She cast an accusing glare at Hunt.

"Most folks say squirrel tastes like chicken anyway, so I figured I might as well fix the real thing."

"Chicken fricassee!" Cullen exclaimed. "Now that's some French I understand."

Cullen grabbed a long-handled spoon, served Gillian a hearty portion, then did the same for himself. Hunt suppressed a grin as he took the bread basket, unfolded one corner of the warming towel and offered her the basket.

"Hot biscuit, Gilly?" Hunt mimicked his brother.

"Ms. Moore or Gillian on the grounds of Moore House, please."

She waited until he nodded agreement and then gave her attention to the meal before her. He was right. The tempting aroma won her over before a morsel had even passed her lips.

"Oh, Chef," she mumbled with her mouth full. "This sauce is incredibly silky."

"I thicken the sour cream sauce by whisking in an egg yolk."

"It's decadently rich." She closed her eyes, savoring the flavors.

"Believe it or not, this is my light version—no heavy cream."

"Well, I'm sold."

"That's what I hoped you'd say. I'll make it a featured item on my menu." Hunt smiled and winked at his brother, a signal between the two.

Gillian paused in her feeding frenzy to consider what had just occurred. She rested against the chair to settle a heart that thumped hard in her chest. She'd unwittingly fallen for an impromptu tasting and been drawn in completely by her talented and wily chef.

She'd expected to *discuss* the menu with Hunt and, when absolutely necessary, to defer to his experience. But Gillian hadn't intended to fall under his culinary spell so quickly or in the name of chicken fricassee.

It seemed her earlier fears about trusting the man were well-founded.

CHAPTER SIX

ON THE DRIVE to Temple Territory the next day, Hunt prepared himself to be in the doghouse with Gillian. He'd called twice that morning, and it'd gone to voice mail both times. Yep, he was on her bad side, he just wasn't certain why. She'd enjoyed the meal, cleaned her plate and even agreed the fricassee was a dish worthy of his menu.

Correction. *Her* menu.

"I gotta stop acting as if I'm running this show," he muttered to himself. "That's probably why she took off before I got a chance to serve the crème brûlée."

In fairness, she had come in the door last night making noise about having to work later that evening. But it was just as likely the hotel heiress had to report to her daddy as to how she was spending his money. Hunt could just imagine her observations—the East Texas locals were slow as molasses in Minnesota, and as easy as shootin' fish in a barrel. Flash some cash and these folks will go along with anything.

In Gillian's mind, setting up shop in this quiet little town would be a sure thing.

Hunt snapped his fingers.

A sure thing. That's the boss lady's Achilles's heel!

She thought her money was the silver bullet, the solution to every problem. Well, it wouldn't buy loyalty or respect. And it wouldn't buy the one thing she needed to succeed in these parts: the hearts of the local folks.

By the time the Jeep's wheels crunched on the asphalt of the private drive, Hunt's mind was humming with a question. Did he dare exploit Gillian's weak spot in hopes of getting her to give up on her plan?

And if he was successful? Then what? He'd put together a group of investors. That's what.

He pulled alongside a new Silverado with local plates, then poked the keys underneath the cracked seat of the old Wrangler and headed toward the stucco mansion. Voices drifted from the kitchen into the high-ceilinged vestibule where Gillian said she planned to install her guest registration desk. A low voice rumbled, punctuated by female laughter. Hunt quickened his steps to investigate.

"So we're in agreement, ma'am?"

"I believe we are," Gillian responded to a tall guy in jeans and cowboy boots. The square shoulders beneath the chambray shirt were familiar, but it was the double cowlick on the crown of the auburn head that gave the visitor's identity away.

"Karl Gates, you redheaded stepchild, is that you?"

The man spun around with a wide smile and stepped into Hunt's bear hug. They held on in friendship, slapping one another on the ribs harder than necessary to see who'd release the embrace first.

"One of you is going to break a bone if you don't knock it off," Gillian intervened.

"What are you doing here, man?" Hunt held his best high school buddy at arm's length.

"I could ask you the same thing, Temple. Thought you dumped us to live in some country where they eat slugs and fish eggs and call it fine *quee-zeen*."

The common sentiment, that he'd *dumped* his old friends to be a celebrity, stung. But that was why he had come home. To put things right.

"Believe it or not, people eat that stuff just up the road in Dallas."

"That's exactly why Cathy Ann and I don't go any farther than Longview for a night on the town."

"There are some adventurous eateries in Longview, my friend."

"Well, the most adventure I want on my plate is a porterhouse from Bubba's House O' Beef, if you know what I mean."

Hunt faked a shudder of disgust, then moved his attention to Gillian. "Should we post a guard at the street to keep riffraff off the property?"

"Mr. Gates is here at my invitation."

"Is that a fact?" Hunt wondered how this turn of events might figure into his new plan. Karl could be helpful throwing a wrench in Gillian's works if he was willing to cooperate.

"Yep." Karl seemed pleased. "Imagine my surprise when Miss Moore called the office this morning and asked us to take a gander at what she wants to do over here. Dad sure is tickled to bid on the job. Updating the woodwork in this big old house will put some extra guys on the payroll. And right here before the holidays, they really could use the work."

"Gillian, do you want me to take it from here?" Hunt offered.

"No, thanks. Mr. Gates and I spent the past couple of hours walking the rooms for the first phase of restoration, and he understands what I have in mind."

Karl lifted a yellow legal pad from the gaping, scarred ledge that had held a deep porcelain sink decades ago. He tucked his notes under his arm, clicked his pen, slipped it into his shirt pocket and then covered his cowlicks with a straw Stetson. Gillian took the hand he offered, and the warm smile they exchanged made Hunt the odd man out.

"Miss Moore, I'll have drawings and samples to you by the end of the week."

"Perfect. I'll make a decision as soon as all the bids are in. I'd love to award the work to a local carpenter, but the financials have to be right."

"We won't disappoint you, ma'am."

Gillian's infernal cell phone buzzed. She pulled it from her pocket, then asked, "Hunt, would you mind showing Mr. Gates to the parking lot? I should speak with my father right now." She faced the other direction so her daddy would get her full attention, which was more courtesy than she'd given Hunt's calls that morning.

He waited until they were clear of the house before he ventured past general pleasantries with Karl. "So let's hear all about your meeting with the boss lady."

"That's a woman determined to get what she wants, if you know what I mean."

"And you agree with her ideas?"

"Not entirely, but my job is to please the client."

"Well, mine is to keep her from destroying the history of this place, and I intend to do it. I want to review what you draw up before you present it to Gillian."

"Oh, I'm not so sure about that, Temple." Karl tugged off his Stetson and slapped the brim against his thigh. "This is business, and I can't afford to screw it up. I can add up the number of mansions being converted into hotels around here on one hand. One finger, actually. This town ain't anything like the places you come from."

"I come from Kilgore, same as you," Hunt reminded his old friend. "And how do you expect she heard about you? I got your foot in the door, didn't I? You can count on my vote when the bids are all on the table. I don't want a crew from Houston up here any more than you do, so work with me, okay?"

"Yeah, okay." Karl climbed in the cab of his pickup, slammed the door and propped his elbow on the open window sill. "How come you're home again? I thought you wanted to get out of Dodge and lose the town gossip about your family for good. You're the *Cowboy Chef* now."

Karl mocked the title. "What do you want with us?"

"Hey, can't a guy come see his brothers without everybody being suspicious?"

"I guess so."

"And it seems I got here in the nick of time. I've gotta keep this place from becoming a No-Tell Motel. And you're going to help me, my friend."

"I'll do what I can." Karl put the key in the ignition and the engine rumbled to life. "So what's up between you and Ms. Moore? Are you just letting her foot the bill to accomplish what you always said you wanted for this old place, or is there something personal going on?"

"What makes you ask either question?" Hunt kept his voice light. "I only met the lady a few weeks ago and you make it sound as if I'm taking advantage of her."

"Well, you ought to at least get to know her better, and fast. That woman's a looker. And when word gets around the Piney Woods that there's a rich, single woman in Kilgore, she's gonna have to fight men off with a stick, if you know what I mean."

He winked and headed his truck toward the exit.

Karl was right. Gillian was beautiful in a fresh way, but she was all business. Hunt doubted the men of Rusk County had much of a chance against the stick she carried. It doubled as a whip.

GILLIAN WAS JUMPY, as if somebody had slipped a double shot of espresso into her cup of decaf. She was well aware of the source of her case of nerves, and it was chemical, all right, but it wasn't her body's reaction to caffeine.

It was that blasted Hunt Temple.

The man was getting under her skin, and she was pretty sure it was by design. The question she'd wrestled with all night was whether or not to do something about the attraction she had to him. The timing was completely wrong, but when would it ever be right? They were both in the hospitality business, a world that required around-the-clock availability. When and where would she ever find a more compatible or attractive man who just might understand the demands of her life?

And if she won him over, he'd become an ally instead of the snake in the grass she was fairly sure he was being when she was otherwise occupied. Staying one step ahead of him with so much on her plate was wearing Gillian out, and the project was only just getting started. The months ahead would be rewarding. She was building her dream. But they would also be the most critical of her life.

If she wasn't so dependent on him to get Moore House off to a great start, she'd save herself a lot of trouble and just fire him on the spot.

"So, are you thinking of firing me?" Hunt asked as he reentered the room.

"You're not only an excellent chef, you're a mind reader."

"I beg your pardon." His head snapped back as if she'd popped him on the chin. "You're firing me?"

"No, just considering it."

"What's that supposed to mean?"

"Well, why did you ask?"

"You went around me and called the friend I told you about. Does that mean you don't want my help?"

"Hunt, what is it going to take to get through to you on this subject? I own this property. Temple Territory is going to become Moore House. You can roll with the punches or punch out. I will meet my opening deadline, with or without you. So which will it be?"

Hunt folded his arms, turned about-face and seemed to study something outside the window. His white knit shirt stretched tight across solid shoulders, revealing the body of a man who could have played professional baseball, if everybody who ever mentioned him to her was to be believed. Those powerful arms could definitely swing a bat.

Or hold a woman close.

Maybe she'd been hasty. What if he walked away? She'd be out more than an executive chef.

Oh, knock it off. Don't let your emotions get in the way of your plans.

"Well, what's it going to be?" She stood

her ground, silently praying he'd stay the course while her nails dug little half-moons into her clenched fists.

"I might ask you the same thing. What's it gonna take to get through to you that I start what I finish?"

"You must admit you've left more than one attractive position."

"But I never left an employer high and dry. I always gave notice and worked at one hundred percent of my ability until the last meal was served. I'll do the same for you."

"That's admirable, and I appreciate you being straightforward with me." The tension in her fists eased. "So, other than putting out exceptional food, what are you hoping to accomplish for the duration of your contract?"

"My first goal is making sure Alma and Felix have a future here with you. They've given their lives to my family, and they deserve security for as many years as they want to continue to work."

"You're covered on that one. What's next?"

"It's no secret that I hope to preserve as

much of the history and heritage of this place as possible." He dropped his chin and held both palms outward. "Yes, I realize it's going to be Moore House, a boutique hotel with a European atmosphere. But you're still in the Lone Star State. There's no way to get around that fact, and I don't understand why you'd want to."

"I don't! I didn't buy property in Texas to pretend I was in France."

"Then make the most of what you bought, for crying out loud." Hunt motioned for her to take in their surroundings. "You have to admit, Pap didn't exactly build a barn. He may have put a few country touches here and there. But as with the saloon doors and the kitchen pantry, every part of the outdoors that he brought inside has its own story. Capitalize on that, don't plow it under like last year's soybean crop."

She released a heavy sigh. "You're right. I'm just so caught up in my preconceived notion of how Moore House would appear that anything beyond my mental image becomes a threat."

"I don't expect you to change what you

have in mind. I'm only asking that you give more consideration to the details before you toss them out as unimportant."

"Throwing out the baby with the bathwater," she mused.

"Precisely."

Gillian stepped forward, more boldly than she was on the inside. She laid a hand on the forearm that Hunt still held crossed against his body. Her fingers pressed gently on the warm skin and his muscle tensed beneath her touch.

"Thank you, Hunt."

"For what?"

"For caring enough about the future of this place to prevent me from shooting myself in the foot. It would be easy for you to stand by and let me make mistakes, wait for me to fail and then clean up after me for a fraction of my investment."

"Hmm." He pressed his lips together in a thin line. "Now that you mention it…"

Gillian jerked her hand free of the personal contact, made a fist and jabbed Hunt hard in the biceps.

"Ouch!" He buffed his palm against the

spot where she'd landed her punch. "You hit like a guy."

"Thank you. I'll treat that as a compliment."

"Treat this the same way."

Hunt placed his palms on Gillian's shoulders, slid his hands down to her forearms, gently gripped her elbows and tugged her to his chest. She should resist, but she didn't. She leaned into him, and his body was warm against hers. She tipped her head back so she could see his face. His eyes were closed as he lowered his mouth to hers. He gave her a lingering but tender kiss and then released her from his hold.

She stepped away, embarrassed that she'd allowed the intimacy, and confused about why he'd taken the liberty.

The aggravating man smiled.

"Well, now that we've kissed and made up, how about if you show me all the woodwork details you talked over with Karl today, so I can help make sense out of his bid when it's delivered?"

She studied his lips as he spoke. If that

was a make-up kiss, then his grudge kiss must be spectacular.

Could the man who'd been quasi-hostile to her only days before now become a respected, even enjoyable guide on this journey?

She'd been suspicious of him up until now, but perhaps it was time to find out.

CHAPTER SEVEN

"This waiting is driving me up the wall!" Gillian stated.

Hunt reached for the French press and filled their cups. Gillian sat across the kitchen table from him, a pen wiggling nervously above her ever-present spiral notebook. Coffee in Cullen's kitchen had become Gillian and Hunt's late-morning routine since they'd declared a truce. A verbal truce, at least, though Hunt had done nothing about his intent to sidetrack the efforts of his boss. Still, guilt niggled him constantly.

"It's only been a couple of weeks. Did you really expect permits to be issued overnight?"

"Evidently I did," she admitted. "I covered so many bases in advance but never considered investigating this business of city approvals. It makes no sense that we can't even begin demolition for minor renovations, much less break ground on new structures. What if they turn me down, Hunt?"

"That's not going to happen." He tried to soothe the blond beauty whose feathers were perpetually ruffled.

"Then why is it taking so long? Inspector Watkins said he'd do his best to hurry my applications through the process."

Hunt chuckled. "I doubt his idea of 'hurry' is the same as yours. City inspectors don't get excited over much, apart from the occasional ice storm that results in a day off."

"I'm going to call down there again this afternoon."

"What do you mean, *again?* Have you been pestering the city's permit office?"

"I'd hardly refer to keeping a tight rein on my project as pestering."

Hunt considered this news. Gillian was a pit bull on a bone when it came to the details. Her ability to focus was critical in a host of positive ways during the start-up of a business. But it could get her tail in a wringer if she needled the wrong clerk.

She was putting the same pressure on her contractors. Karl complained that she was on the phone with him at least once a day, and the work hadn't even begun yet. How would Gillian act once the property was crawling with crews? Could she step aside and let them do the work she was paying them for, or would she be up in their business, questioning every detail?

By all indications, if left to her own devices, Gillian would implode before the first frost. He didn't have to do anything to derail her plan. She was doing it herself. It should have made him happy, but somehow he didn't relish the idea of watching her fail. Still he reminded himself she didn't have as much to lose as he did.

Meanwhile he was making quiet inquiries into funding in case Temple Territory went back on the market. After Gillian trampled every toe in town and made her retreat to the security of corporate life, he'd be ready to step in and make an offer to the bank. Pap's place would end up in the family after all. Hunt would restore and remodel the kitchen and dining room, but the rest of the mansion would remain as his grandfather had intended; a memorial to the life of an independent Texas oilman. So what if people still claimed Mason Dixon Temple was crooked as a dog's hind leg? J. R. Ewing was no better, and he was as big a legend as Hunt's real life namesake, the great H. L. Hunt.

"So what do you suggest I do instead?" Gillian asked. "Wait patiently and let the holiday season come crashing down on my head?"

"What's the worst that can happen if you don't open the doors in December?"

Her eyes couldn't have been any more incredulous if a horn had sprouted from his forehead. "I can't believe you're asking that question, as if missing the deadline were an option."

"I'm not insinuating it is, but you're sitting here with too little to keep you busy and too many people to pester, so I'm asking you to consider the worst-case scenario and get it over with."

She dumped a heaping teaspoon of raw cane sugar into her cup and stirred as if her life depended on it. She couldn't make a permit materialize, but by golly she would make those crystals dissolve.

"I can't even consider that possibility."

"You mean you won't."

"No, I mean I can't. There's more at stake than I'm willing to admit out loud. The consequences of failure are even steeper than the rewards of success."

She dipped her chin toward her chest. A curtain of golden hair swung out from behind her ear, hiding Gillian's face from his view. She must have struck a heavy bargain with her daddy to be so worried about the outcome of her first business venture. Naturally she wanted to do well, but it wouldn't be the end of the world if she didn't. She was an only child. If her parents had been willing to bankroll her once, they'd do it again. And again.

"*Buenos días,* Miss Gillian and Mr. Hunt," Alma greeted as she came through the door. Hunt jumped to his feet to help with the bag she carried. Fresh mustard greens sprouted from the top of the re-cycled shopping sack Alma filled almost daily at the farmer's market.

"Buenos días, señora," Gillian responded. *"¿Cómo es usted?"*

"Muy bien! You've been practicing," Alma said, complimenting Gillian's efforts to learn some phrases in Spanish.

"It only took a few days in Texas for me to figure out a crash course was in order."

"These greens are almost as pretty as you," Hunt teased Alma as he sorted the contents of the bag, appreciating her eye for the freshest produce.

"This one is the sweet-talker of my boys." Alma pretended to share a secret with Gillian. "He will have you eating from his hand and twisted around his pinkie finger."

Hunt wrapped Alma in a hug from behind. He towered over the short woman, pinned her arms to her sides and lifted her feet off the ground. "How am I supposed to stay ahead of my new boss if you give away my secrets?" he hissed.

"Put me down, you bully." Standing on

her feet again, Alma tugged at the hem of her navy housekeeper's dress. "I'm sure this pretty lady has figured out for herself that you will say anything to get your way."

"That's only with you, *Mamá Pequeña,*" he said, calling her by the name she loved, Little Mama.

Gillian wondered how accurate Alma's statement was. Hunt hadn't done anything more to cause his loyalty to be questioned, nor had he made any further effort to kiss her. But he was definitely clear on who buttered his bread.

"Hunt's being honest, Alma. He hasn't tried any lines on me that I'd categorize as sweet talk."

"Give him a while longer." Alma winked, and then went about the job of rinsing and storing her fresh vegetables.

Hunt took his seat at the table again. "Thanks for speaking up for me, Gillian. You'd expect her to be prejudiced in favor of her youngest. Instead she's always expected the worst from me."

"What I expect from you is to put those cups and saucers in the dishwasher and

then get out of my kitchen. It's a beautiful fall day. You kids go outside and play."

"She's right. Let's not waste this perfect
weather. How about a drive out to Lake
Cherokee, Gillian? I'll show you where my
brother Mac lives and we can have lunch
at the marina."

"Under one condition."

"That's a shock." He squeezed his eyes
shut, as if the condition would be painful.
"Go ahead, name it."

"That we stop by the courthouse on the
way through town to check for word on
my permits."

"You're going to irritate those folks if
you're not careful." He slanted a warning
look her way.

"Thanks for the advice on interpersonal
skills, Dr. Phil."

"Just consider yourself forewarned."

"Hey, you have to break a few eggs to
make an omelet," she reminded Hunt.

"You've got me there."

SITTING IN THE passenger seat of Hunt's ancient Wrangler as they cruised the shore

of Lake Cherokee seemed oddly natural to Gillian.

"My father had a Jeep when I was a teen-ager," she mentioned above the growl of the engine.

"Did he teach you to drive it?"

"No, it was a model with a history of rolling over, and he didn't want me behind the wheel. He taught me in Mother's Lincoln."

She remembered the mammoth sedan they'd bought secondhand and driven until the wheels had fallen off. Her mother had always been partial to gas-guzzling land yachts. But Dad said she put in so many hours, either behind the front desk or filling in for the catering office when they were short-staffed, that she deserved the comfort of a big luxury car. It was their one indulgence as they socked away money for the future. Her no-nonsense father had been raised to save and he'd taught Gillian the same strict discipline. Living well within her means had become second nature, so the extravagant spending on Moore House was nerve-racking.

Every day that passed without moving closer to opening the doors was a waste of twenty-four precious hours. She used them as wisely as possible, but Hunt made a good point. If she continued to pressure everyone she came into contact with, she'd get a reputation for being difficult. Even if she had good reason for earning that reputation, it would make business harder down the road.

"Well, what do you say?" Hunt pulled the hand brake.

"About what?" She'd tuned him out a few miles ago.

"McCarthy's place?" He pointed toward a two-story A-frame home that perched on a ledge beside the four-thousand-acre lake. The house was designed from deep red cedar, huge panes of glass and chunks of ruddy-colored rock. The view from inside had to be breathtaking.

"Your oldest brother's done very well for himself."

"Mac's the mathematician in the family, a natural bean counter. He did his best to guide the rest of us to use our inheritance wisely, but he's the only one who really parlayed his money into a serious nest egg."

"The inheritance you received when your parents died?" She'd done enough research to learn his folks had gone down in a private plane when the boys were all probably still in school.

Hunt leaned forward and crossed his forearms over the steering wheel. He nodded. "Pap had died years earlier when natural gas caused a rig to explode in West Texas. But Daddy didn't find out about it till long after the fact when an old friend of Pap's came through Kilgore and stopped for a visit."

"Nobody notified the family that your grandfather had been killed?" Gillian was mortified.

"Nope. My dad and grandfather hadn't spoken in years. Dad wasn't even sure where Pap was living."

"How sad. Do you mind telling me why?"

"Pap was convicted just as our dad was applying for college. The state took everything they had, and since Dad was already eighteen there wasn't even a provision for his support. He was forced to leave Temple Territory and move in with neighbors to finish his senior year or go stay with his mother's people in Georgia. He'd never even met them, and they didn't exactly welcome him with open arms, since they assumed he was somehow messed up in Pap's dirty business dealings."

"I'm sorry to keep prying, but what was your grandfather convicted of?"

"Drilling slanted wells." Hunt made an angular motion with his hand. "A lot of wildcatters were doing it, and plenty of people were aware of the practice. Slant-well drilling was a way to get even with the major oil companies for squeezing out the independents."

"That's a Robin Hood way of thinking."

"Sort of, justifying the crime didn't make it right. Others were charged but Pap was the only one convicted. His foolish refusal to fill his wells with cement to hide the evidence of his crime cost him fifteen years of freedom."

"What happened to your father when his dad went to prison?"

"He stayed in Kilgore, got into college and worked three jobs to support himself. After he married my mother, she helped to put Dad through medical school, and he agreed to come home to practice in order to get grants from local businesses.

"By the time Pap was paroled, Daddy was in private practice at the only hospital in town. He and Mama had four young'uns and a life of their own, so Pap went quietly out West. My dad got a letter from the Texas Department of Corrections saying Mason Dixon Temple had been paroled, but Pap never got in touch, and my folks left it alone."

"What did your parents tell you boys about your grandfather?"

"They didn't have to tell us much of anything. The town made sure we heard all the old stories and probably a lot besides. I asked my daddy once why he didn't change our name and move away from the gossip, and he said, 'What my Pap did will hurt like the dickens for a couple of generations, and then people will forget. We'll make our own name. This is our home, and we're not going to run away.'"

"Then your grandfather's friend just dropped by out of the blue?"

Hunt nodded. "Wilbur was one of Pap's roughnecks on Temple One back in the day. They met up again out in West Texas and worked together until Pap was killed. Poor old Wilbur had no idea he was breaking the news when he told Daddy how sorry he was about Pap's death."

"How did your father deal with it?"

"Not aware his Pap had died and not even knowing where he was buried gnawed at Daddy in ways you can't even imagine. But he was determined to honor the old man's wishes and keep the rest of us clear of the shame. Pap took it to the grave with him, and that's the way he wanted it."

Hunt stared past her toward the lake that could be seen beyond his brother's magnificent home. The wind gusted whitecaps on the water that lapped at the shoreline.

"Did you ever meet your grandfather?"

"Nope."

"That's just tragic." The sentiment was heartfelt. "When did you find out about Temple Territory?"

"I can't remember ever not being aware it was Pap's place. It was the only part of the story that we boys could be proud of when kids said we were a family of thieves."

"Children can be so cruel."

"Adults can, too, and unfortunately the memories here are still sharp. That's one of the reasons the property's been empty for so long. The story that Temple Territory is jinxed kept locals from wanting to invest in it."

"So that first day when you said the place was cursed, you weren't just making that up to scare me off?"

Hunt leaned his head against the seat and laughed.

"Oh, I probably said it to scare you away, but I didn't have to make it up. Remember, this is Texas. The truth here is bigger and stranger than the whoppers anywhere else."

"And the legend of the Caddo well? Was that story just to scare me, too?"

"No, ma'am." He shook his head, once

again serious. "It's never been proven, but the Caddo believe that hole was dug by their ancestors whose spirits still haunt the well. Pap respected that, and I do, too."

"That nasty thing stinks."

"The supernatural usually does." He sounded ominous.

"You can't really believe that story." She brushed him off. He was messing with her head.

"The descendants of the ancient tribe believe that the spot is sacred. Pap honored their superstitions by preserving the well, and if you're smart you'll leave it just as it's been for hundreds of years."

"Or what?"

"You watched the film *Poltergeist,* didn't you? I wouldn't want to be around when you find out the hard way that Pap was right."

CHAPTER EIGHT

To GILLIAN'S RELIEF, the building permits began to trickle in by the end of October. Serious work finally got underway but it was out of order. Things were happening, just not according to Gillian's carefully conceived plan.

She started each day full of hope that she'd make progress, and then fell into bed at night beneath the weight of more stress than she had ever imagined possible. Six weeks into the renovation and she was constantly second-guessing herself. Maybe Hunt had been on to something when he'd tried to get her to consider the worst-case scenario. Plan A was not coming together, and there simply was no plan B.

Either Gillian was failing or what the locals said was true: Temple Territory was jinxed. Either way, it would be fatal. And after her father's call a few hours earlier, she wasn't sure she would bear up under another blow.

"Miss Gillian, would you come approve this molding before I sign off on the delivery and let the guy unload?"

"Sure, Alberto," she agreed. She followed the foreman of Karl Gates's team to the area where building supplies were being staged. A flatbed had been backed up near the temporary Quonset barn that shielded construction materials from the elements. The truck driver in his familiar orange apron waited with his clipboard for a signature.

"Is this what you and Mr. Karl agreed on? I expected the crown to be eight inches wide." Alberto slid a length of wood forward for Gillian's inspection and laid a tape measure across the width. "This is only four."

"Please tell me you're joking." Even before Gillian got her hands on the molding, she realized this was no laughing matter. The custom order was half the width they'd expected. This material, arriving two weeks late, would never give the ceiling the illusion of a French drawing room. She took aim at the innocent driver, her last nerve shot.

"Get your boss on the phone," she demanded.

"Um, ma'am, I don't carry a cell. Can't afford it."

She stomped toward the open door of the flatbed, reached inside and yanked the built-in microphone off its dashboard mount. "Is there someone on the other end of this thing?"

Anxious eyes looked to Alberto and then back to Gillian. The driver nodded his head in response.

It took all the composure she could muster not to shoot the messenger. She stretched the chord to its fullest extent and thrust the mic toward the driver. "Get your dispatcher on the line and inform him the lady who owns Moore House is beyond furious!"

"Moore House?" he questioned.

She blew out a sigh when a scream was really what she wanted to let loose.

"Temple Territory, then. Tell them the

lady who is remodeling Temple Territory is, to put it in local terms, madder than a wet hen! And as soon as it is humanly possible, Mr. Gates will be at your store with some choice words for the idiot who screwed up my custom order."

To Gillian's horror, her throat began to thicken and her eyes burned from emotion that wouldn't be held in. She ducked her head, brushed past Alberto and made a beeline for the mansion. Once inside and up the staircase, she closed herself into the sitting room that served as her on-site command center. With no one to see and no reason to fight away the tears, she let them flow.

HUNT RECOGNIZED A golden opportunity when one smacked him upside the head. He'd watched from the Jeep as Gillian and Karl's foreman hurried out the terrace door. They'd examined the load on the delivery truck and then Gillian had pitched a hissy fit. He could have made things more embarrassing by stepping into the scene before she fled inside, but that pesky niggling kept him frozen to the spot.

He'd come to this moment with a clear conscience, but it would never be clear again if he didn't do the right thing now. One day soon he'd succeed in his own right, he was sure of that in his heart. But it wouldn't be at the expense of a hard-working, hardheaded woman who was determined to give her all, even if she went down in flames in the process.

"Aw, man," Hunt muttered as he crossed the parking lot and motioned for the delivery driver to give him a minute.

"I didn't hear exactly what Ms. Moore said to you, but I got the impression there's been a mistake of some sort. I apologize for not stepping in sooner to deal with the problem myself, but if you'll give a copy of the purchase order to my friend Alberto, I'll call your store and get this all straightened out."

He fished a five from his wallet and thanked the driver for his patience, then patted Alberto on the shoulder.

"I got this one," Hunt assured the foreman.

"Thank you, Mr. Temple." Alberto smiled his appreciation.

Hunt passed through the downstairs rooms, admiring the progress being made by the carpenters and painters. Gillian was stressing big time, but things were shaping up. True, there were large-ticket items running behind, and the crews were working around holes in the schedule, but it wasn't out of the question to imagine the work finished well before Christmas.

He'd even considered stringing holiday lights on the derrick out front, and positioning a lighted star atop the hundred-foot structure to match the sixty other replica derricks in town. But none of that would happen if he didn't convince Gillian that she wasn't a failure and get her to ease up on the throttle.

"Gilly?" he called as he rapped on the closed door of the room where she'd set up her office. "Gilly, are you in there?"

The door flew open.

"I asked you not to call me that around here. I don't want the men to get the wrong idea." She left him standing in the hallway.

Hunt followed and pushed the door closed again. He settled into a folding chair next to the makeshift worktable that she'd put together with plywood and sawhorses. Why she chose this setup when she could easily afford a proper desk was beyond his understanding.

"What wrong idea? That you might be human and a nice lady who can take a little teasing on the job?"

"That's not what I was thinking."

"Then maybe it's time to change your mind-set," he suggested.

"Meaning?" She took the other chair.

"You will catch more flies with sugar than you will with turpentine."

Gillian blew her nose on a tissue and tossed it into the five-gallon bucket that served as her trash can.

"So I'm supposed to simper and sashay and pretend to be a helpless Southern Belle so people will say I'm sweet?"

"How many women have you met in Kilgore who sashay, for cryin' out loud?"

"I haven't looked that closely."

"Well, add the effort to your to-do list.

Maybe it'll help get your mind off yourself, and you'll start to appreciate the town you handpicked for your new home."

It was good advice, and he should probably take it himself.

Her head angled away, moist violet eyes narrowed. "Since when do you consider this *my home?*"

"Since you knocked out a few walls, brought in a load of river rock to build a fireplace in the restaurant and started fitting every room on the first floor with new baseboards and crown molding."

At the mention of the molding her lips popped open like a largemouth bass after a water bug. He sensed that round two of her hissy fit was coming, so he held his palm up to prevent the flood of words. "Yes, I've heard all about the delivery guy you threatened to strangle with his own radio chord."

"I wasn't that bad," she argued.

"I witnessed the whole thing, Gillian. When you realized he'd brought the wrong order, you threw something out there in the parking lot that was just short of a conniption."

"All right, I did!" She grabbed the nearby roll of architectural plans and smacked them on the plywood for emphasis. "And with good reason."

She brandished the roll of drawings as if they were a sword for defending her honor. "The devil is in the details, and if they aren't handled properly, then nothing that comes next will work."

Hunt stood and extended his open palm. "You've only shown me the plans for the first phase of the ground floor. Let me see the rest so I can understand what all the fuss is about."

She snatched the roll close to her chest. "This information is on a need-to-know basis. When I decide you do, I'll share it with you and not before."

Hunt leaned over Gillian, placed his hands on her shoulders and bent so close that her metal chair tipped back on two legs. She held tight to the plans, refusing to be intimidated by his nearness. He dipped his face to hers and let a threatening smile ease across his lips.

"Give me the drawings or give me a kiss. It's your choice."

Her lovely eyes widened in defiance. Her gaze locked with his. The chair rocked, unsteady, as if it might tip over. Gillian's hands flew out for balance. She let the plans drop to the floor, but she never let her eyes lose contact with his.

Was it possible that his nearness was more important than her precious drawings? Hunt's heart raced. He wanted to kiss the woman. Rather badly. But not without her consent.

Hunt stepped away and let the front legs of Gillian's chair thump to the floor. He stooped, retrieved the roll of paper, handed it to her and then returned to his seat.

"Why are you playing those cards so close to the vest?"

"Because what I plan to do next is still entirely on paper, and I'm not ready to share it. I'm in over my head as it is, and you'd probably try to talk me out of it if you saw what I have in mind."

"I deserve more credit than that," he complained.

"You do, Hunt." She leaned forward, reached across the space between them and placed her palm on his knee.

Her tender touch was warm. "You've become a friend, and I'm not sure I'd have gotten this far without your advice, even though I haven't asked for it as often as you've given it."

She smiled to mask the blunt point.

"Well, prepare for some more."

Gillian dropped against her chair, ending the brief physical contact. "I'm not up to your veiled criticism right now, Hunt."

"Even better, because there's no time for candy-coating."

"Whatever bitter news you're determined to deliver will have to wait. My father called this morning with some tough news of his own, and I'm up to here with worry." She gestured to the space above her head.

He leaned forward. "What's the matter?"

"He and my mother will be here in a few days, and things have to be on track before they arrive."

"Aah, coming for their first visit to see how you're managing their investment."

"I wish that was all there is to it." She shook her head miserably and reached for a tissue.

As she dabbed at the corner of her eye, Hunt realized the impossible was about to occur. That stiff upper lip of Gillian's was beginning to tremble.

"Is whatever's got you so upset also on a need-to-know basis, or can you can tell me what's going on?"

"I might as well. You'll figure it out when they show up and never leave."

"Huh?"

"They've been laid off," she said quietly. "Both of them."

"What do you mean, laid off?"

She huffed out a breath and rolled teary eyes. "You've heard about it on the news. It's that thing companies do when they have to cut costs?" The sarcasm was watered down.

"How do you get downsized out of your own business? Who gets laid off from a place that belongs to them?"

The misery on her face morphed into confusion.

"Where did you get the idea that they own the hotel where they work?"

"Different things you've said gave that impression."

But had she really planted the idea with her words, or had he jumped to the conclusion to suit his own purposes? The huevos ranchero Alma had prepared for his breakfast rumbled in Hunt's belly as a fresh supply of acid in his gut punctuated Gillian's news.

"If I did, then that was my bad," she accepted the blame. "I never meant to imply anything other than the fact that my parents are hardworking people who've given their lives to one employer. Only now it seems their positions are redundant, and they're being forced to take early retirement."

"So they're coming here?"

She nodded, not at all pleased.

"Dad and Mom are shell-shocked. They've decided that the best way to get past the blow is to take on a new challenge.

They want to help out, 'stay busy,'" she mimicked her father.

"And you object to that because…" He struggled to grasp why she wouldn't be excited to have her parents nearby. The Temple Brothers would have given anything for another day with their folks. The judgmental thought must have shown on his face. Gillian had the grace to flush with shame.

"It must be hard to grasp. But you'll understand once they're here and you see how much of my personality comes from my father."

"So, he's bossy, too?"

"Oh, you have no clue. That's why he's been successfully running a hotel for so many years. He manages every detail, and he's constantly correcting everybody about the way they do things."

"Yep, you're a chip off the old block."

"I have spent my entire life trying to stay a step ahead of him so he won't be on my case. But if he comes in here and starts being unreasonable with my contractors and crews, this place is going to experience a mutiny."

"You realize the potential for mutiny already exists, don't you? And you can't blame your daddy for that situation."

"It's that serious?" She winced.

"You know the answer to that, Gilly. I understand how important this is to you, but you're inflicting a load of stress around here and making yourself crazy in the process."

She ran both hands through her hair, catching strands of blond in her fingers and resting the beautifully tangled mess atop her head. His fingers itched to touch the silky tendrils that hung free.

"Nothing is the way I'd imagined it would be, Hunt. I'm not sure how to adjust."

"If you get a bushel basket of broccoli instead of the cauliflower you ordered, you switch recipes and make the best of it."

"Yeah, yeah, I get it. When life gives you lemons, make lemonade. That's clever when it's embroidered on a pot holder but not so useful for me right now."

He took closer note of the dark smudges beneath her eyes.

Gillian was miserable. Off balance. Not the pretty powerhouse who kept everyone else on their toes.

His heart raced as he decided what his next move should be. One wrong step and he could put his foot in it for good. But would she be the one to pay the consequences? And could he live with himself if she got hurt?

CHAPTER NINE

"GILLY, DARLIN', TELL me what you want from me so I can help. Shoot straight, 'cause I don't wanna make the situation worse."

She sat up taller in her chair, did a first-rate job of appearing pulled together and in control, but he'd already seen the weakening in her tough exterior. As many hours as Gillian spent with that infernal cell phone to her ear, it was never for anything other than business or to argue with her daddy. Right now the woman needed a friend. A close friend.

"How can I help you?"

"Why would you even ask that question?" She sniffed. "I'm just fine on my own."

"Oh, come on. Give me some credit here." He indulged in the exaggerated eye roll she'd been leveling at him for weeks.

"I made the conscious decision to partner with you instead of treating this situation as if it were a hostile takeover. And as difficult as it's been, I've kept my hands to myself, for the most part, when what I'd really want to do is..." He stopped, refusing to give her the pleasure of hearing him say more.

If she wanted to hear how he felt about her, she'd have to work for it.

She paused. Taking the bait, no longer on the verge of tears and once again sassy, she asked, "What you'd really want to do is what?"

"To put you over my knee. Your daddy obviously didn't do that often enough, no matter how tough you say he was on you."

"That's not what you were about to say," Gillian challenged. She left her chair, moved in front of him and leaned down with her hands on his shoulders as he'd done to her minutes before.

"That is exactly what I meant to say. When you are frustrated, you behave a little like a child. And while I, personally, think it's somewhat charming—"

Gillian leaned closer, and he felt her warm breath on his cheek. He finished, "—the rest of the people who come in contact with you find it to be shrewish."

She snapped to attention, and her posture became finishing-school perfect. "Shrewish?"

He nodded, dipped his chin and kept a grin to himself.

"Why didn't you say so before now?"

"Oh, right. You've already shared your irritation with my unsolicited advice. It would have been about as popular as a roach in your grandma's potato salad if I'd mentioned it might be a good idea for you to sweeten up your method of dealing with people."

She slumped down in her chair, folding her arms in a defensive posture. "Sounds as if you've thought this over."

"Yes, ma'am, I surely have," he drawled in his best Texas accent. "You've got the skill to be a charmer—you've used it on me, though not nearly enough. If you'd flex your charm muscles more often, you'd have everybody you come in contact with eating out of your hand."

"That's not my style," she insisted, stubborn as always.

He considered for a moment, then looked her up and down.

"Have you worn your hair that way all your life?"

"Of course not." Gillian grimaced before adding, "I hate to admit it, but ten years ago I had a curly perm."

He couldn't hold back a smile at the image of Gillian with corkscrews. "Why don't you have those curls today?"

"Because styles change, and you have to change with them or be labeled a fashion dork."

He pretended to aim an imaginary pistol and pull the trigger. "Bull's-eye! You change with the circumstances. That is, if you're smart."

"Okay, I get the point," she conceded.

"There you go, darlin'. I was sure there was a savvy woman deep inside that sizzlin' hot body."

It was easy to admit but harder every

day to remember that the oh-so-appealing exterior belonged to his boss lady.

GILLIAN LOOKED AROUND at the changes, unable to believe her eyes. What a difference three days and countless man-hours made! With a few kind words and some expensive overtime, she'd been able to convince the local electricians and plumbers to work around the clock to ready several suites.

She moved from the hotel to the upstairs area she'd been using as her office space and powder room, enjoying the creative distraction of cobbling together country-chic accommodations for herself and her parents.

"I couldn't have done all this without you, Hunt." Each day her gratitude toward him increased, though he always brushed off her words of appreciation.

"Kindly keep that sentiment in mind when a paying guest sends her overcooked and underseasoned snapper back to the kitchen," he challenged.

"Ah, you remembered," she crooned, as

if he'd recalled something endearing. "How sweet."

"No, it's just good business to pay attention to what people say about your work."

"And what do you expect my father will say about the place so far?"

Hunt glanced around the suite her folks would occupy.

"Be honest," she insisted. She was satisfied with what they'd accomplished in a few days, but she wanted a man's perspective.

"What you've done with these rooms is pretty impressive."

Gillian had been aching for his reassurance. Without fear that Hunt would judge her actions, she moved close, and his strong arms instinctively encircled her body. He cradled her head in his hand and pressed her cheek to his chest. She heard his heartbeat, a thumping as strong as her own. She boldly tilted her face upward expecting to find his lips. Instead, Hunt sought the skin at her temple where he pressed a lingering but tender kiss.

"Thank you," he murmured into her ear. "I haven't had a hug in a long time."

"Me, either." She squeezed him harder for covering her awkward neediness and then ended the embrace.

"So you don't believe this room is too rustic?"

"Maybe for some parts of the country, but not for Texas. And the fact that you found most of the furnishings at local salvage and resale shops makes it extra special. I suspect you're planning to go French country up here with the rest of the guest suites, but you ought to model some of the rooms after this one."

"I hadn't even considered spinning a local thread, but you make a good point. People don't expect to find Danish modern in Lincoln's bedroom when they visit the White House."

"And when they come to Texas, they want a taste of the Lone Star State in their accommodations, because they're gonna get European in the restaurant."

She gouged him in the ribs with her elbow.

"Ouch!" He rubbed the spot. "Cullen's been goosing me that way all my life."

"Where do you think I got the idea?"

"That's it. No more meals for you at his house."

"Speaking of meals, I've got my parents' suite covered, but there won't be a working kitchen for a while yet."

"That occurred to me, as well. The walk-in cooler will be installed next week, and that'll help with breakfast and lunch, but until then you'll have to eat out."

"Where shall we take them tomorrow night?"

"We? Don't you want to spend the first evening alone with your folks?"

"There will be plenty of time for that. I'd be forever grateful if you could run interference with my father when he starts in about the construction delays, at least for the first night."

"I've got you covered." He nodded with certainty. "And why don't you let me take care of dinner tomorrow? You meet their flight in Dallas and when you get here, I'll be available to help with the grand tour and their first meal, Texas-style."

There was a dangerous glint in Hunt Temple's eye. She hoped they wouldn't arrive at Moore House to find a side of beef on a barbecue pit in the front yard.

CAR DOORS SLAMMING and loud barking announced the arrival of the newcomers. Hunt took one last glance at the work he'd done with Alma's help, drew a curtain closed and made his way to the terrace. His curiosity about Gillian's parents would have to wait, because he had eyes only for the stunning blonde escorting two strangers and a dog from the parking area.

A dog?

A huge black dog with a mop of curly hair loped up the steps. Its pink tongue was the only distinguishing feature in the twilight as it cut like a racehorse from one point of interest to another, investigating at will.

"Heel," a gruff male voice commanded.

"He's okay, Dad. Let him wander."

"I believe it's safe to presume you are

Mrs. Moore." Hunt extended his hand to the lovely woman who could only be Gillian's mama. "But who is this guy?" The dog was sniffing his boots with great interest.

"That would be Cooper," Gillian's father answered, also shaking hands with Hunt.

Gillian made introductions and then explained that James and Meredith Moore had brought along their standard poodle that was perpetually in need of a haircut, making him resemble a Portuguese water dog.

"It seems we're going to be a pet-friendly hotel."

"Honey, I'm sorry, we should have asked."

"It's okay, Mom, really. *Mi casa es su casa,* which makes it Cooper's *casa,* too."

"I beg your pardon?"

"*Casa* is Spanish for home." Gillian smiled at Hunt, and he sent her a quick wink. "You'll catch on fast, trust me," she assured her mother.

"Well?" Gillian swept her hand toward

the mansion. "What's your first reaction to Moore House?"

"It's spectacular," Meredith complimented the structure, and then took in the view of the private lake. "I see why you fell in love with it at first sight."

"I want more detail on why this place has been on the market without a buyer for so many years." James sounded skeptical.

"Sir, I'm well acquainted with the details, and I'll be happy to share them with you over dinner." Hunt deferred to Gillian. "Ready to give them the grand tour?"

"Such as it is, yes," she agreed and led the way.

Just inside the door Hunt had set up a table to serve cocktails.

"May I pour you a glass of wine?" He offered the label for the inspection of Gillian's father, who nodded curt appreciation for the award-winning California vintage.

Hunt made a mental note to replace the bottles he'd taken from Cullen's collection but probably with something easier on his wallet. He removed the cork and poured expertly, aware that Gillian was watching him closely.

"You did that like a pro." She accepted the crystal stemware.

"I paid attention during sommelier class. It was more interesting than turning potatoes," he said, reminding her of the day she'd poked fun at his Cordon Bleu credentials.

"We were relieved when Gillian said you'd accepted the executive chef's position," James shared as he sniffed his wine. "Having you on board will lend credibility to Moore House as we establish ourselves in the first few years."

Hunt waited for Gillian to steer the conversation, unsure whether or not her parents were aware his contract was only short-term. It wasn't his place to share the details, though, so he played along.

"Shall I show you the work that's been done so far?" Gillian changed the subject and began her guided tour through the rooms on the main floor.

She pointed out architectural details Hunt had never noticed, even though he'd assumed he was the expert on Pap's place. Her knowledge of the work that had already been done and the work that was still to be accomplished before the holidays was extraordinary. It wasn't necessary for him to run interference with Gillian's father; she was entirely capable on her own.

The realization caused heat to wash over Hunt, and he recognized the warm discomfort for what it was.

Shame.

While he'd slept peacefully at night, she'd been awake studying and analyzing every detail, and certainly every penny spent. She was a competent business-woman, and here he'd believed he could run her off simply by shaking her confidence. He'd convinced himself that his support mattered to her, but she could do it all without him.

And without the approval of her father, if necessary.

As they moved toward the dining room, Gillian began to make excuses for the mess caused by the masonry work still in progress. Her flow of words ended when she noticed the curtain, which was really a couple of bedsheets, precariously strung across the entryway. The dog poked his head underneath and then settled on the floor as if waiting for the big reveal.

"Hunt? What's this all about?" Gillian's brows quirked at the surprise.

"Your daughter bravely left dinner up to me," he explained to James and Meredith. "I figured the least I could do was serve you your first family meal right here at Moore House."

With a little flourish he swept the curtain aside. Gillian followed her parents into the space that had still been filled with construction materials when she'd left hours before. If she hadn't covered her mouth with her hand, the delighted gasp might have become an excited squeal.

Hunt's heart melted.

"You made it sound as if it was a wreck in here," Meredith commented to her daughter.

"Oh, Mom, it was an awful mess. There was rock and dust everywhere, and the wall above the fireplace was only half-completed." She linked her arm with Hunt's and gave him a smile that caused his insides to lurch. "This is all Hunt's doing."

"I had a lot of help from our stone masons, and my brothers did the cleanup. I finally found a use for those guys."

Hunt placed his hand over Gillian's and led her to the table covered with white linen and set with his own dear mother's best china and silver. He seated Gillian as James seated his wife, and then Hunt took the empty chair for himself. The mismatched sheets that covered the entry to the kitchen were pushed aside by Cullen, dressed in makeshift waiter's garb, as he stepped into the room holding a serving tray just as he'd been taught.

By his little brother, of course.

This was Gillian's dream, and he could give it to her tonight. And tomorrow, he'd see about finding his own dream.

CHAPTER TEN

CANDLELIGHT FLICKERED.

Shadows danced on the unpainted walls and freshly grouted stonework.

To Gillian, the aroma of recently sanded wood floors was as heady as Hunt's masculine cologne. The cozy and quiet atmosphere in the cavernous room was amazing, but she had come to expect amazing from Hunt.

After the endive salad, she excused herself and made a quick trip to the kitchen where she found Alma prepping plates for the main course. Cullen was still in the dining room regaling her parents with stories of growing up in a house full of boys, so she helped sauce the perfectly grilled veal chops.

"Shoo, Ms. Gillian." Alma made sweeping motions with her hands. "Get into the dining room before Hunt catches you touching the plates and wrings both our necks."

"He is a little funny about people messing with his food, isn't he?"

"He gives Mr. Cullen a hard time over the obsession with books, but each of my boys has his own brand of OCD. When Hunt was still in high school, he threatened to eviscerate his brother McCarthy for putting ketchup on a glazed duck breast. Now *that* was funny."

Gillian snickered and gave Alma a quick hug. But before she rejoined the others, she whispered, "Alma, forgive me for underestimating you when Hunt first suggested I hire you to be my chef."

Alma waved away the apology. "I am not a trained chef like Hunt. I am just a cook with a lot of years' experience feeding the Temple family."

"The experience you have can't be taught in a fancy French school. Hunt cooks from talent, but you cook from love."

"Thank you, Ms. Gillian," Alma accepted the compliment, and then pointed toward the curtain. "Now, go!"

"Yeah, go on ahead," Cullen agreed as he entered the kitchen, his tray filled with empty plates. "I left little bro on the hot seat, but he's doin' a fair job of holding his own." He smiled and gave Gillian a thumbs-up.

"That's quite a tale," her father was saying to Hunt when she returned to the table.

"We wish it was just a tale, sir. Unfortunately the details I shared with you are true, but I grew up hearing a lot of embellishment from the folks of this town. So take my version to the bank and take the rest with a grain of salt."

Cullen came out again, moving about the table with the main course.

"Were you embellishing that first day about when you said local Native Americans have tried to lay claim to the property?"

"Oh, no, that business about the Caddo Nation is a hundred percent accurate." Cullen just had to put in his two cents' worth. "Enough artifacts have turned up during excavations in the area to prove they were here centuries before the white men. Like most tribes, they don't have any legal rights to the land they were driven away from, but that doesn't stop them from staging a sit-in every now and again. You'll see." He winked at Gillian.

"I don't care for the sound of that," James said, concerned.

Gillian glared at Hunt over the linen napkin she used to dab her lips.

Hunt took the hint. "Sir, my brother's yankin' Gillian's chain."

"Am not," Cullen protested. "Every square inch of Texas was inhabited by somebody else until the Spanish Conquistadors came onto the scene in the seventeenth century. At one time, France, Spain and Mexico all laid claim to this land before the Republic of Texas and the Confederate States were formed. It wasn't until after the Alamo and the Battle of San Jacinto that it belonged to the settlers. And even then, they had a long row to hoe to hang on to it."

"Are there legal ramifications that my daughter hasn't considered?" James said to Hunt.

"Not any more than there are in your neck of the woods," Cullen interrupted again. "The Virginia Indian Territories were inhabited for thousands of years before European colonization. You really can't blame Native Americans if they kick up a fuss now and again. Protest just comes with the territory."

"Thanks for the history lesson, professor. You're excused," Hunt muttered to his know-it-all sibling.

"This meal has been amazing." Meredith changed the subject. "And I'm most certain there's a wizard on the other side of that curtain whipping up dessert. But I'm going to have to take a rain check, or ask for a doggie bag. We've had a very long day, and it would be nice to settle in to the hotel where we'll be staying."

Gillian stood and both men rose, as well. "Come with me, Mom."

"Hunt, will we see you tomorrow?"

"You'll see me every day. I may be the executive chef, but I'm also part of your daughter's crew. If she wants it done, I do it."

"Well, then, good." Meredith smiled, as lovely as Gillian.

The two ladies left the dining room with the unconventional-looking poodle in close pursuit. Hunt watched them take the grand staircase to the second floor, grinning because he knew what was waiting at the top of the landing.

"Something funny?"

Hunt wiped the grin off his face. "Not so much funny as happy. Your daughter's gone to a lot of trouble so you and Mrs. Moore will be at home here. I'm sure you'll both be pleased."

"She's always worked hard." James scowled, brows drawn together as he stared in the direction the two women and the dog had gone. "Even with her head in the clouds, Gillian accomplishes more than most people I know. I just hope that, when it's all said and done, she won't bankrupt us over this decision to come to Texas. There were perfectly good properties closer to home, but no. It had to be her way or no way."

Hunt studied Gillian's father, searching

for signs of his daughter beneath the hard exterior. She was definitely a chip off this old block, albeit a kinder, gentler chip.

"Mr. Moore, I've always staked my claim to this place because it belonged to my grandfather. But all those years I was all talk and no action. I planned and schemed, but I never did anything to make it happen. Then your daughter came along, smart and decisive, and she jumped on this property like a chicken on a June bug. And she made it happen. There's a lot to be said for going after what you want."

"This is more akin to going over Niagara Falls in a barrel. Maybe she should have started smaller, been less ambitious." James gave a disapproving shake of his head.

"Sir, forgive my impertinence, but if you're not confident in Gillian's plans, why are you bankrolling her?"

"She's my daughter," he answered quietly. "And I love her."

"I'm not sure she's aware it's that simple."

"Of course she is." James folded his napkin and placed it beside his empty plate. "I have to get our bags from the car. When Meredith calls it a day, she rarely changes her mind."

"Sounds like her daughter."

"Oh, yes. Gillian is her mother's child. She didn't get anything but the color of her eyes from me. We're not the least bit similar, as you can probably tell."

Hunt waited for James to smile, acknowledging that his comment was tongue-in-cheek. But he didn't. The man seemed to have no idea that his daughter was opinionated, tenacious and driven, her father made over.

"HUNT, THANK YOU for everything you did last night. Mother was so impressed." Gillian's voice drifted from the cell phone speaker as she shared her parents' reaction to the country-chic suite upstairs.

As he listened, Hunt stepped into a favorite old pair of Lucchese boots. He tugged the legs of his starched jeans down smartly, checked to see that his plaid dress shirt was tucked in neatly and then appreciated the effect in the full-length mirror. At the moment he seemed more like a cowboy than an executive chef, but that image had become part of his allure in the fine-dining business. The reason he'd been dubbed the Cowboy Chef.

Every famous chef had a signature. And while Hunt was building a reputation for his skill in the kitchen, his Texas drawl and boots had become his trump cards. Today he was dressed to play his ace in case that's what it took to get an offer from the premier steak house in Manhattan. His agent had done the legwork by setting up the meeting, and now it was Hunt's job to move the deal into negotiations.

"Hunt, did you hear me?"

"Yes, of course, sorry. I'm dressing and have to be out the door in a minute."

"Is there any chance you could bring some of Alma's sopaipillas with you?"

He picked up the cell and punched off the speaker feature. "I don't have the time, but Alma will be glad to bring them over. As much as I hate to do it, I have to fly to New York for the day. I'll be home very late this evening."

"Oh." There was disappointment in the single word. "The walk-in is being delivered, and I just assumed you'd be here to oversee the installation."

"I'd planned on it, but something's come up. I'll call Karl on the way to DFW and ask him to keep a close eye on the kitchen. And I can stop by on my way in from the airport tonight to check on how things went, though I don't want to wake your folks."

"Hunt? Is this trip about a job offer?"

"It's too soon to say. I'm going up to talk to Rudy Owens about the direction he's taking his steak house chain next year. The flagship store is in Manhattan, and I want to see for myself how it operates."

"Sounds like the perfect opportunity for you. Good luck." The encouraging words contrasted with her flat tone.

"You and I have a contract, Gillian. Moore House can count on me to stay the course no matter what comes out of today's meeting."

"Moore House appreciates the reassurance. Have a safe trip." She ended the call.

The excitement he'd been enjoying since he had spoken with the Manhattan restaurateur wilted faster than spinach on a hot skillet. He'd let the prestige of the invitation overshadow his gut sense that going to New York would be wrong, akin to cheating on Gillian. But that simply wasn't the case. There was nothing personal between them. Not yet, anyway.

And she should put the money she was wasting on an idle chef to better use getting ready for a holiday season opening at Moore House. Even the name had stopped creeping him out. Hunt had begun to accept the fact that Gillian's vision and drive were transforming the old wildcatter's mansion into a boutique hotel worthy of royalty. Pap would be proud. And one day the gossip might finally die down for good.

Maybe it would be best if he got out of Gillian's way and let her succeed without his involvement. Because as long as he stayed in Kilgore and associated with Moore House, the local folks would assume it was all his doing, not Gillian's. That might have appealed to him a few weeks before, but in this morning's light, it seemed downright deceitful.

Hunt glanced at the bedside clock. He had to get started on the two-hour drive to DFW where he'd catch his flight, though he'd prefer getting a root canal to getting on a plane. The cell phone was still in his hand. It would be so easy to punch the redial key, get Rudy back on the line and say he'd reconsidered, wasn't interested.

But just last night Hunt had confessed to Gillian's father that he'd been all talk and no action for far too long. What man worth his salt would continue on that path? And what woman would want him on those terms?

Hunt tucked his cell into the case clipped to his belt, grabbed his keys and headed for the Jeep.

CHAPTER ELEVEN

IT WAS WELL after midnight when Hunt pulled onto the road that led up to the mansion. An inviting glow was still visible from several windows on the main floor as he pulled into his usual spot. Pap's place shone brightly, a beacon on the hilltop. Hunt took a moment to admire the repairs to the exterior stucco finish and the new coat of paint that reminded him of fresh cream. He'd have kept the original white, and he'd have been wrong.

Moore House was lovely, just like her mistress.

The terrace doors swept open and a black phantom moved swiftly across the tiles, bearing down on him, a stalker on its prey.

"Cooper, stay," Gillian called softly.

The shadow stilled and a pink tongue

drooped from between gleaming white teeth.

"Hey, buddy," Hunt spoke, hoping the dog would find his voice familiar. Cooper bounded forward to accept scratches behind his soft ears. "Are you up this late all alone?"

"This sweet boy's been keeping me company."

"Burning the midnight oil, huh?"

"As usual. Come on inside. It's too cold to stand out here for long."

"Yep, it's fall in East Texas." He followed Gillian through the French doors with Cooper close behind. Hunt paused to secure the lock and when he turned around, he stepped into a warm hug.

GILLIAN WRAPPED HER arms around Hunt and tilted her face up to his, determined to show him her heart before it was too late. He seemed hesitant, but returned the unexpected embrace.

"Whoa, this is a cozy welcome even for such a chilly night."

His voice was different. Maybe it was already too late.

"How did things go today?" he asked.

"You first."

Hunt let his arms slip away, took Gillian by the hand and pulled her toward the kitchen. "Let's see the new work while we talk."

The room was ablaze from the recently installed overhead lights. It was exactly what he'd requested, and Gillian agreed it was perfect for a professional kitchen staff.

"This certainly explains the glow I saw from the highway when I entered the property. Nice." He walked around the spacious kitchen, his head tipped back to appreciate the new fixtures. "I wondered if you'd downgrade what I'd put on the requisition."

"Why would I buy less than what you requested?" A state-of-the-art kitchen was important to Gillian, and she'd assumed Hunt felt the same.

"Oh, just to shave some cost," he explained. "I certainly understand any decisions you have to make to come in under budget on the project as a whole. It's not as if the kitchen should take priority over the guest rooms."

He hadn't seemed concerned before now, and this change of heart was unsettling. Had he been needlessly driving up her costs with pricey items, or did the quality of the surroundings not matter any longer because he didn't plan to stick around? She led him to the walk-in cooler and pulled the heavy door wide.

"Did you expect me to downgrade here, as well?"

"Wow!" His mouth gaped open like a child seeing his first carousel. "You got the Big Mac Daddy?"

"Hunt, this is what you said we should have," she reminded him.

"In the restaurant business, the equipment we *should have* and the equipment we can afford aren't always one and the same." He tested the strength of the racks that lined one wall, smiling at the quality of the materials. "This is first class all the way, Gillian."

"I repeat, what made you think I'd purchase anything else?"

He stopped ogling the equipment, closed the door and turned his attention to her.

"I can't speak for the hotel industry, but let me share the cold hard facts about fine dining." He took her hand and pulled her close. Gillian shivered as he slid his arms around her waist. "Is this okay? I don't want to get into trouble with the human resources department."

She nodded and smiled, giving him approval to continue.

"Eighty percent of new restaurants go belly-up in the first five years. That failure rate is one hundred percent of the reason I haven't gone out on my own before now. If I had the funds, which I don't, I'd buy everything secondhand and cut corners wherever possible, so I could invest my money in the food and the service. Focusing on what I put on the plate and how well I care for my diners would hopefully allow me to stay in business against the odds."

"Hunt, the rest of our new appliances are being loaded on a transport truck as we speak. Isn't it a little late to be sharing this financial wisdom with me?"

"You never asked for my guidance on how to spend your money. In fact, you've cautioned me on more than one occasion about sharing my unbidden point of view on any subject. Besides, as I just said, I don't know squat about owning a boutique hotel and you do, so I figured your opinion was best."

"You figured right," she said, determined to sound confident. "I did my homework. I visited places that gave me complete access, probably the sort they gave you at that restaurant today. I have journals full of notes on everything from the thread count of the sheets to the brand of coffee they serve to the paper quality of the comment cards they mail to guests. I studied customer feedback and rankings and, yes, I'm aware of the failure rate for the industry. I've accepted that there is no sure thing, no guarantee. But there's timing, creativity, hard work and prayer, and I have all that in spades."

"That, pretty lady, is true." His arms tightened as he pulled her closer. She felt the warmth of his breath in her hair. "I didn't mean to cast doubt on your professional progress, just to explain away my lack of the same."

This time Gillian was the one to ease free of the embrace. She'd worried all day, and now she had to hear the worst. "Well, you must have made some progress today, so tell me about it."

"Is there anything to drink in there?" He nodded toward an insulated cooler Gillian kept stocked for the construction crews.

She raised the lid, reached into the melting ice and retrieved a bottle of blue energy drink. "It's still cold."

He took the container, twisted off the cap and drank deeply of the funky-tasting stuff the workers seemed to love.

"Aah," he exhaled. "My daddy would say, 'Better than beer and almost as good as whiskey.'"

"You must have been doing a lot of negotiating to be so parched."

A happy grin spread across his handsome face as he began to share with her his experience at the Manhattan restaurant where he'd spent the day.

"The business model is a proven success in New York, Chicago and Atlanta. Rudy wants to open three more stores this year, and he said I could take my pick of Austin, Denver or San Francisco."

An odd sensation thundered beneath her ribs. She wasn't sure if her heart was racing or shutting down. Either way it was scary. And it hurt.

"All three of those are great cities, so it'll be hard for you to choose." She worked at projecting a calm she didn't possess.

"I haven't decided if I'll take the offer, but it's a nice one to have on the table, since this place will be up and running before you know it."

How was she going to confess that she hadn't corrected her parents' mistaken impression that Hunt was staying on indefinitely? When her father had mentioned it, she'd steered the conversation away from Hunt's contract, hoping against hope that he would decide to hang around Kilgore a while longer.

"When do you expect the folks you hired in Virginia to start making the move?"

"My events planner has been working remotely, setting up a hush-hush wedding and reception for December. She says she might have to stay in D.C. if she can't lease her home, but we can work around that situation. But my manager of housekeeping should be down later this week to search for a home and start interviewing for her staff."

"I should get busy doing the same thing, especially if you believe a big deal is in the works. I'll make sure we get off on the right foot before I seriously consider Rudy's offer."

"You're going to accept it, aren't you?" Her voice quivered.

She lowered her eyes to avoid Hunt's, but he brushed his knuckle beneath her chin, lifting her gaze to meet his. She saw his answer before he spoke the words.

"Gillian, it's what I do for a living, and it's what I love. I have to consider my long-term finances, and you can't afford to keep me on indefinitely."

"I'll be the one to decide what I can and can't afford. You said yourself that once word gets out, our restaurant will be *the* venue where everyone wants to book parties and special events. Your name and reputation is already part of my marketing plan." It wasn't yet, but she'd go in that direction if Hunt stayed around.

"How's that?"

"The deal that's in the works for December was sold with you as the secret weapon." Not true, but what could it hurt to stroke his ego a bit? "An East Coast celebrity couple wants to reserve Moore House exclusively for three weeks, so they can have privacy for their wedding. The price is steep, and the promise of the Cowboy Chef is the reason they're about to sign the deposit check."

"You make me feel so cheap," he teased.

"Trust me, there's nothing cheap about this booking, and it's the perfect vehicle to get Moore House in the press. Once the media gets wind that this couple has said their vows in an exclusive little hotel in East Texas, there will be national coverage on every network."

"I'm intrigued. I guess I'd better start

planning a special wedding menu and contracting a bakery for the cake."

"Exactly. Set all thought of running a steak house on the back burner for now, please. It's critical for my executive chef to put his kitchen in order and pull out all the stops for an event that will rock the Big Rich of the Texas social scene."

"I'll start tomorrow," he agreed. "We'll put on a wedding worthy of the bravado that built Temple Territory."

Gillian didn't react to the name or try to correct him. Instead she breathed an inward sigh of relief to have Hunt on board, at least for the short term.

CHAPTER TWELVE

GILLIAN HADN'T EXAGGERATED about the social status of the couple who would be married at Moore House in a few weeks' time. The aging but still stunning runway model and her former bad-boy rock star had been living together and raising a family in the public eye for as long as Hunt could remember. The fact that they were finally going to tie the knot would be huge news in the entertainment business.

The arrival of Gilly's parents hadn't been part of her plan, but they'd been a godsend. While Gillian and Hunt put their heads together around the myriad of details for the event, James dogged the renovation crews, as she'd warned he would, and Meredith took point on decorating the guest rooms. She loved the rustic theme that Gillian had used in a pinch, and the women had decided to carry it throughout the other ten suites upstairs.

"Bless your Pap for having the foresight to build bathrooms en suite," Gillian commented as they toured the rooms and admired the updated plumbing fixtures.

Hunt laughed at the memory of a story his father had shared years before. "Pap took Dad to the old home place once. It was way out in the Piney Woods where there is no such thing as indoor plumbing. Pap grew up having to walk about fifty yards to use the outhouse in every possible kind of weather. He swore it would be different when he had his own home, and he made good on that oath."

"How nice for me that your grandfather was scarred for life by his childhood experience!"

"I never fully appreciated that story until just now," Hunt admitted as he passed his hand through a motion sensor that triggered the flushing mechanism.

"So may I use the outhouse story in the history-of-the-mansion brochure?"

"Brochure?"

She smiled shyly, as if she had a surprise up her sleeve.

Not so long ago Gillian had been clear that what Hunt had to share might be worth considering but wouldn't necessarily sway her decisions. But these days his input seemed to matter. The realization warmed him against the chill in the house. To hold down preopening utility costs, they kept the thermostat low upstairs.

"I've been making notes of all the details you've shared with me about the property, and I've organized them into a storybook of sorts. It's amateurish at the moment, and I want to see a prototype before I decide whether or not to continue, but it might be a nice take-away for guests."

She definitely had his attention as they made their way to the next suite. He couldn't help but appreciate the fit of her wool slacks as he followed close behind.

"It sounds intriguing." He made an effort to keep his mind on the conversation.

"So, may I use the outhouse story?"

"Be my guest. Nothing I've shared is a family secret. In fact, all the Temple skeletons rattled out of the closet before I was born, so I'll be interested to see what you consider interesting enough to put into print."

"I'm glad you don't object to me using some of your anecdotes."

He shook his head. "Not at all. But I must admit I'm surprised you want to be so public with the history of the property. You've always seemed determined to let Moore House develop its own persona instead of resting on the dubious laurels of Temple Territory."

"Don't get a big head over this, but you've changed my mind about more than a few things."

He let his eyes widen and threw his hands up in mock horror. "You don't mean it. I said something of note and you paid attention?"

She smiled at his joke, the violet of her irises deepening.

"I'm always listening. Even when you're yammering on about minor things just to distract me from my work. It may not be undivided, but you have my attention."

"For instance?" he fished.

"For instance…" She pointed toward the large window. "That patch of bent grass on the south lawn that your grandfather planted to impress the snooty golfers who never invited him to the country club."

"That was a corny little detail that I shared the first week you were here. I'm amazed you even caught the mention."

"I try to take note of everything that might be useful."

"Well, take note of this."

Hunt scooped Gillian close and captured her mouth. Any concern he might have had that she'd resist melted as she leaned into his body, returning his ardor. He savored the long, slow kiss he'd been imagining for weeks.

"Smooching in an empty guest room has gotten more than one couple suspended from my housekeeping staff," Meredith interrupted from the open doorway. Cooper's feet bounded across the wood floor and he poked his nose between them, demanding a group hug.

Gillian responded to her mother's voice

as if she were a teenager caught kissing on the front steps in the dark. She spun around, running one hand through her hair while the other smoothed the front of her tailored blouse.

"You look fine." Her mother smirked.

"Sorry about that, Mrs. Moore," Hunt apologized, stroking the insistent dog.

"Sorry about what you were doing, or sorry you got interrupted?"

"Oh, definitely the latter," he admitted with a smile.

"You're both way over the age of consent, and it didn't appear to me that anybody was in distress, so I suppose I'm the one who should apologize for barging in."

"Mom, it's okay. Did you need something?"

The unusual pink fluster in Gillian's cheeks was charming. Hunt could imagine a dozen more ways he'd enjoy putting the blush there again.

"No, I was just making notes for my trip over to Canton tomorrow."

"Oh, that's right. The big trade market is this weekend." Hunt had meant to suggest he and Gillian make the trip together, but Meredith had the jump on him.

"I'm driving the rental box truck over there and I hope to bring it home full of side tables and accent pieces. I've furnished lots of hotel rooms in my day, and this is so much more fun than purchasing mass-produced items from a catalog."

"Canton is one of the best regional flea markets in the country. If you take cash, you'll do well."

"Why don't you kids come with me?" Meredith slipped her arm around her daughter's shoulders and gave her a reassuring squeeze. "Gillian, you've got impeccable taste, and I could use another pair of eyes. Hunt, your strong arms would be a huge help to haul purchases to the truck. What do you say? The forecast is for perfect weather, and I hear it's a lovely drive."

"Mom, there's so much to get done. I can't afford a day away."

"Nonsense. Your father will make any decision that needs to be made, whether he's asked to or not. And I suspect you haven't taken a day off in all the weeks you've been here. Am I correct?"

He sensed Gillian hesitate.

"Yes, ma'am, you hit that nail right on the head," Hunt answered for her. "Except for one afternoon ride out to the lake, she hasn't seen much of the countryside."

"Well, it's high time you got out among the locals. When in Rome, as they say."

GILLIAN COULD STILL feel the heat in her neck and face from Hunt's kiss, and it wasn't entirely due to being caught by her mother. Spending a day with the two of them would be way too *normal*. And normal was a condition she couldn't get used to, especially now that Hunt was bound to go his own way after the holidays. Best not to let her guard down so low that her heart got bruised. She'd take a pass on the outing, and that would be that.

"I'm in," Hunt enthused. "What time do you want to be on the road?"

"I checked the GPS, and it's a little over an hour from here. If we leave at seven, we can stop for breakfast on the way and be there when the gates open."

"I don't think…"

"I have a better idea," Hunt talked over Gillian's objection. "I'll make breakfast to go and you ladies can eat while I drive. How's that sound?"

"I'm not sure…"

"That's an offer we can't refuse. I can manage a truck when I have to, but I'd just as soon enjoy the scenery from the passenger seat."

"Then it's a plan," Hunt agreed, an endearing smile on his face as he conspired with her mother.

The two seemed pleased with their decision, though Gillian hadn't said she'd go along. She considered her options. She could be a martyr and refuse on the grounds she was too busy. She'd spend the day butting heads with her father and end up regretting her decision to stay behind. Or she could be swept into their enthusiasm. What would one day hurt?

They looked to her for agreement.

"Okay," she gave in. "But only if you

make breakfast burritos with Alma's handmade tortillas. Extra chorizo for me, please."

"Extra everything on my order," her mother chimed in.

"Done. And I'll bring plenty to feed your husband, so he won't be left out of the fun."

Meredith waved away the concern. "I asked James to go with me, but he turned the invitation down flat. That man would much rather watch paint dry than be trapped all day at an antiques market."

"Then he should be a happy camper with all the paint drying at Moore House this week," Hunt observed.

"Now that everybody's on board with the arrangements, I'll get busy building my shopping list and let you two get back to… whatever it was you were doing when I interrupted." She gave an exaggerated wink and left with Cooper at her heels.

Hunt checked his watch. "I'm meeting with a prospective head waiter this afternoon. This guy has experience as a line cook so he can double as kitchen staff when we're shorthanded. He might even make a good chef one day, if you appreciate his food."

Her spirit sank at the reminder that Hunt was already searching for his own replacement. He was being practical, but it was too soon for her to consider the possibility of losing the man who had become an important person in her life.

And in her heart.

"Can you stay a bit longer, Hunt? We should talk about what just happened."

"You mean with your mother?"

"Well, yes, and what we were doing when she showed up."

"And what was that? I don't recall," he teased.

She narrowed menacing eyes his way.

"Oh, now I remember." He moved close, pulled her into an embrace and bent his lips to hers.

"Hunt, I'm not sure this is such a good idea." Even to her ears it lacked conviction.

"Because somebody else might see us, Gilly darlin'?" He crooned the question, his voice a low rumble.

"No, because somebody right here in

this room might get emotionally involved." She stared into his gray eyes, telling him with her gaze what she couldn't admit with words.

"Somebody right here in this room might already be emotionally involved," he confessed. Was it possible he felt as vulnerable in this situation as she did?

"Exactly. And the possibility already exists that your career will take you in another direction very soon. Is it wise to go down this dead-end road?"

"So what if it is a dead end? Can't we enjoy the journey for as long as it lasts? Ours is a demanding business. We work when the rest of the world eats, parties and sleeps. Sharing free time, such as it is, with another person in hospitality makes sense, don't you agree?"

"It makes sense in my head. I'm not so sure my heart will agree once you make up your mind to leave."

"How about you let me worry about what's up ahead, and you worry about what's right here, right now?"

"That seems pretty shortsighted."

"Maybe so, but the here and now is really all anyone can count on. I'm just suggesting that we enjoy the moments we have together today and that we let tomorrow take care of tomorrow. Can we do that?"

While Hunt's philosophy was appealing, it was also frightening. But what choice did she honestly have in the matter? She could encourage Hunt to pursue an offer and move on with his life, or she could accept things as they were and hope he stayed.

But she'd been planning, making notes and completing checklists since she was old enough to hold a pencil. Could she turn the most critical moments of her life over to chance? Was it possible to let love happen willy-nilly? She didn't even have a section for romance in her planner!

Hunt took her lack of argument as agreement and lowered his mouth to hers.

As Gillian savored the hint of peppermint in his luxurious kiss, she accepted the fact that she was about to let tomorrow take care of tomorrow, knowing she'd eventually have to deal with the fallout.

CHAPTER THIRTEEN

HUNT HARDLY SLEPT that night.

The doubt in Gillian's voice had played over and over in his mind, like a fast-food jingle that wouldn't go away. Something was warning her to keep distance between them, and Hunt suspected she should listen to her intuition. But he was busy trying to convince her to live in the present and let the chips fall where they may on another day.

In all honesty, her way made good sense while his was an emotional roll of the dice. Even Cullen recognized the difference between tenderloin and baloney, and he'd called Hunt on it last night.

"You think it's smart to continue whatever it is you're doing with Gilly?"

"And what is it I'm doing?"

"Come on, little bro. You may be able to

pull the wool over that lady's pretty eyes, but I see right through you."

Hunt dropped all pretenses with his twin and came clean.

"I'm falling in love, Cullen."

Hunt closed his eyes, ground his teeth and braced himself for the lecture that was coming. Cullen would recite all the objections that he could come up with on short notice. But Cullen was biased. He'd never experienced head-over-heels-love. Except for Joiner, whose high school sweetheart had lost her battle with diabetes during their senior year, the Temple men had limited experience with matters of the heart. How could they possibly understand the turmoil Hunt was experiencing?

After several quiet moments with no outburst from Cullen, Hunt chanced a peek at the face that was a mirror of his own. And his brother did the strangest thing.

He smiled.

"That's great, buddy." Cullen was sincere.

He reached out a long arm, hooked his hand behind Hunt's neck and pulled him into a brotherly hug. They thumped each other on the back and mumbled in husky voices.

"Thanks, man. That cuts my freak-out quotient by half."

"Why would you be freaked out?" Cullen's eyes locked with Hunt's. "Isn't it about time one of us had a serious relationship?"

"Sure, *one of us* should do that, but I didn't expect it to be me. Everything about this is wrong."

"Name one thing that's wrong."

"I'll look like a big fat loser." Hunt made an L shape with his thumb and forefinger, and held it to his forehead for a moment. "People are either gonna say I used Gillian to get Temple Territory, or they're gonna say she gave me what I never could acquire on my own. Either way they'll call me a loser. So much for shaking the stigma that goes with our name."

"Are you going to pass up a special woman like Gilly just to rob the old biddies in Kilgore of a day's gossip? The folks in this town have been talking about our family for fifty years, and we've never had any control over what they've said. It won't matter if you settle down here or in Little Rabbit, Australia, you're going to be a topic of discussion. Maybe for once you should capitalize on the notoriety instead of running from it."

"I've never run from anything."

"Haven't you? Why'd you go to school in France when you could have learned everything that was important right here?"

"Le Cordon Bleu has the best reputation," he insisted, well aware the school's U.S. programs were equally well respected.

"Why'd you work all over Europe when the States have become such a great training ground?"

"Europe had better opportunities." But he'd also passed up some great domestic affiliations.

"If that's true, then why'd you take the executive chef job in the Caribbean when you could have been in Amsterdam, or better yet, Paris or Rome?"

"Seriously? You'd choose winter in any of those cities over the beach in Cancun?"

"So why did you quit after one season and come back to Kilgore?"

"Because even if my old friends don't exactly welcome me with open arms, this is my home."

"Exactly. This is your home and everybody knows you as Cullen Temple's inferior twin, not the Cowboy Chef. Some of them feel like you left us in your dust, and you ought to spend some time mending fractured relationships. When you're home, nobody expects or even wants you to live up to that exaggerated Texas persona. Home is where you blend in with the rest of the crazies in hats and boots."

"But I enjoy being the Cowboy Chef and standing out in the culinary crowd. Is that wrong?"

"Nope. And every time you tie that white knee-length apron on over your Wranglers, you stand out among the cowboys and rednecks, too. Trust me. Nobody mistakes you for a forklift driver down at the Home Depot." Cullen held his palms out as if to say *I rest my case.*

"You have the answer for everything, don't you?"

"Not quite, but I do have a few that might make life easier on my little brother. Don't worry about what people think or say, because in a hundred years, none of that will matter. But in a couple of generations, if Pap's place is still up on that hill, owned by your grandchildren, I'd say you and Gilly did well for yourselves."

"This isn't about Temple Territory anymore, Cullen."

"Yes, I realize it's not, and that's what makes me happy for you. That's what makes it right, especially given your weird attachment to the place."

"What do you mean, weird?"

"You don't have to pretend with me," Cullen insisted. "You never did. You may have fooled everybody else when you took to camping with Karl every weekend after Daddy and Mama were killed, but I was certain you two were over at Pap's place."

Cullen was right. Hunt had spent lots of nights in a sleeping bag beside his friend, sheltered in the courtyard beside the Caddo well. He found comfort in imagining that the souls of his parents were somehow nearby, that he wasn't an orphan after all, that the Caddo spirits inside the well were watching over him.

And yet what he'd said to his brother moments ago was true. It wasn't about Temple Territory any longer.

It was about the woman that he loved.

That night, Hunt tossed in his bed as he revisited over and over his conversation with his brother and Cullen's blessing. Finally, in the morning light, though his future was still foggy, his emotions were clear and perfect, like sunrise over a field of bluebonnets. It was too soon to tell Gillian what was in his heart. He needed time to absorb it, and she needed time to catch up. But hours were in short supply, and they were flying by like a whirlwind over West Texas.

He had to make the most of the weeks ahead, and he'd start today. Gillian might be slow to cooperate, but Hunt recognized an ally in Meredith Moore. It was possible the girl who was melting his heart would refuse outright overtures, but Hunt suspected her mama would help him out.

IF SHE DIDN'T know better, Gillian would swear Hunt was hitting on her mother. The two of them had been behaving like high school lovebirds all morning. Hunt was so solicitous that it was sickening. While Gillian hauled herself into the shotgun spot, Sir Galahad handed her mother up into the truck and asked if Meredith was comfortable in the backseat. Then he complimented her on everything from the bandanna she'd tied over her hair to her sensible old boots. Gillian gagged inwardly as Hunt laughed out loud at her mother's stories during the ride over to Canton, as if she were a stand-up comic.

In return, her mother giggled at his stupid puns over the items for sale and asked his opinion of every stick of furniture before she made a purchase. Their egos fed on one another like parasites. If Gillian thought she'd have to fend off Hunt's attention that day, she had another think coming. She might as well have stayed at Moore House for all he seemed to care.

"Are you getting hungry or can you wait a while longer to eat, sweetie?"

Gillian's head snapped toward her mother. Who was she calling *sweetie?* Guilt warmed her cheeks as her mother addressed her again.

"I figured we'd treat Hunt to a nice lunch, but I'm not sure they have anything over at those food trucks to compare with the amazing breakfast he brought us."

"You're too kind." He flashed a grin toward Meredith. "Those were just ordinary scrambled-egg burritos topped off with some of the secret jalapeño salsa I perfected in Cancun."

"If I offer to help out in the kitchen sometime, is there any chance you'd teach me your secret?"

"I'm sure I can be persuaded to give a lesson to a beautiful woman," he agreed. They smiled and bumped shoulders.

"Oh, would you two knock it off," Gillian snapped. "Mom, you're a married woman, and you're carrying on with Hunt as if he's cougar bait."

"I beg your pardon, young lady," her mother said. "Just because we haven't let your sulking spoil our day, that's no reason to be rude."

"I haven't been sulking," Gillian insisted. Had she? She looked to Hunt for confirmation. "Have I?"

He exaggerated a grimace. "I have to side with your mama. You have been kinda cranky since we left the house."

"Well, what did you expect? I warned you last night that I couldn't spare the time for a silly shopping trip."

"And I suppose we should have listened, but you seemed downright eager to join us this morning," her mother reminded her. "But we're here now, so how about if we make the best of this 'silly shopping trip,' as you called it? Let's split up so we can cover more ground, and we'll meet at those food trucks in an hour."

"That'll work." Hunt was quick to agree. "You head that way, and I'll stick with Grumpy."

Gillian elbowed him hard in the side and scowled.

"See?" he pointed out.

"I just have a lot on my mind," she insisted as her mother gave her a quick peck on the cheek and set off on her own.

"Then let's distract you with all this great stuff." He swept a palm outward where row upon row of bargains waited to be discovered.

Hunt hadn't been kidding when he'd said the regional swap meet was a big event. There were acres of items. Everything from homemade wine to imported silver tea services to furnishings straight out of Martha Washington's childhood home, if the hype could be believed. Within their allotted hour they bought two Shaker-style trunks that would double as side tables, and a set of Early American Windsor chairs for the dining room.

Gillian's earlier irritation evaporated as they arranged to have their items delivered to the customer pickup area and then headed toward the aroma of grilled and deep-fried food.

"I can't wait to find out what the food trucks have to offer," she said.

There was a spring in Hunt's step as they approached the lane of mobile restaurants. He caught Gillian's hand and tugged her along.

"I must say I'm surprised. You actually seem excited to eat this stuff," Gillian said.

"*This stuff* isn't the prepackaged deviled eggs and chili dogs from the days of the roach coach. Now you can get gourmet cuisine made to order with all-organic ingredients. Most large cities have sanctioned areas specifically for this purpose now, and they're doing big business. You'd be surprised how many chefs have opted for a truck over a brick-and-mortar operation."

They approached a bright yellow panelvan with awnings raised over open sides and hungry people lined up three-deep at each serving station.

"Hey, I recognize this truck!" Hunt squeezed her hand tighter.

Large letters proclaimed the establishment Wings Across the World. The chalkboard menu offered deep-fried or grilled wings with a list of sauces that resembled the United Nations roster.

"It used to belong to a chef we called Jackpot. If he's still the owner, I'll take a half-dozen Thai and a half-dozen Creole with extra tabasco. Oh, and a jar of his pickled peppers to go. How about you?" Hunt asked Gillian.

She marveled at the childlike excitement that radiated from his face. He'd never been more handsome, and her belly quaked at the memory of their kisses the day before. What chances she might take with him right now, if only they weren't in a crowd.

Gillian blinked to bring her mind into the moment—they were beside a yellow truck at an antiques fair, where her executive chef was actually excited about service from a deep fryer on wheels. But she had to admit, the smells emanating from inside were causing her mouth to water and her eyes to burn.

"Temple! Man, is that you?" A thick Hispanic accent called from the window above their heads. "I'll be right out."

Moments later the rear door of the truck

burst open and the man who'd recognized Hunt jumped to the ground in a tie-dyed T-shirt, acid-washed jeans and rubber flip-flops. With his braided ponytail, he was an image straight out of the sixties.

"Jackpot! I was just telling my friend Gillian here about you." He made introductions.

Friend? The description stung for some reason. Well, what did she want him to say? She wasn't officially his girlfriend, and she'd ordered him weeks ago to stop introducing her as the boss lady.

"If you're friends with this character, you're either armed and dangerous, or you should be," Jackpot teased. He held Hunt at arm's length, and the two men looked one another up and down. "You haven't changed a bit, you ugly dog."

"It's so good to catch up with you, Jackpot. What are you doing in my old stomping grounds?"

"That's right. I forgot the famous Cowboy Chef is from around here." He nodded at Hunt. "These days I spend most of my time in Houston and Austin, but we make this Canton show whenever we can. It's nice to get out of the city, and it's a cash cow weekend. How about you? Except on TV, I haven't seen you since Vegas, and that was nearly three years ago."

"After that cooking competition, I went down to the Caribbean for a while. But at the moment I'm working with Gillian over in Kilgore to get her boutique hotel up and running."

"If you're in the business for something permanent, Rudy Owens is hiring for his new places."

"Yeah, I heard all about his expansion."

"I'm considering the Austin store myself."

"Is that right?"

Gillian imagined the wheels grinding in Hunt's head. This Jackpot person was not only an industry colleague, he was industry competition. Hunt would have to make a move soon if he wanted the steak house in Austin. Worse still, Denver or San Francisco.

"Yeah, the truck's a good living, but it

would be nice to serve my food on a table for a change."

"But then you have all the stress and risk."

"Not if it belongs to somebody else. If Rudy's willing to bankroll the restaurant and let me manage it, that might be just what the doctor ordered. A buddy from Vegas has been working for Rudy for years. Says he's a fair boss who stays out of the kitchen and as long as the profit margins are good, he trusts his executive chef to work the plan."

"You can't ask for a much better deal than that," Hunt agreed.

"Hey, you two." Gillian's mother edged her way through the lines. She cradled a footstool upholstered in blue silk with finely carved legs.

"Nice purchase, Mom."

"I see the resemblance, but this señora is far too young and beautiful to be your mother," Jackpot insisted.

"I hear that a lot," Meredith played along.

"What does a guy have to do to get

some wings around here?" Somebody in the crowd complained.

"That's my cue." Jackpot shook Hunt's hand and bowed to both women. "We're on Facebook. Stay in touch," he called before hoisting himself into the truck and closing the door.

"A friend of yours, Hunt?"

"Yes, ma'am. We met in culinary school in France."

"That guy, Jackpot, is classically trained?" Gillian tried to imagine him in a white chef's coat.

"Don't let the old hippy getup fool you. He struck gold right out of school when he got hired at one of the premier restaurants in Vegas. One night he literally rolled the dice with his paycheck and hit a big win. He quit the restaurant and paid cash for that truck the next day."

"That's why you call him Jackpot?"

"You got it." Hunt snapped his fingers as if he'd just had an idea. "Hey, if Jackpot's interested in settling in one spot for a while, he might consider Moore House. He could park his truck out by the lake and use it for special events, like catering that big wedding next month."

"When pigs fly," Gillian muttered the short reply.

"Hey, this is Texas. Stranger things have happened."

CHAPTER FOURTEEN

THE DRIVE to Kilgore was quiet. Meredith nodded off early in the ride, and Gillian seemed lost in thought, probably making a mental checklist of things to argue with her father about when they got to Moore House. Hunt glanced at the beauty on his right and noted the barbecue smudges on the front of her Redskins sweatshirt. She'd been more agreeable after a generous serving of Jackpot's wings with a side of *pommes de terre frite*—crispy fries dusted with herbs de Provence.

Hunt smiled to himself at the image of his old buddy. The brief encounter was a vivid reminder that today's culinary business was a close community, a small world that the general public had begun to peer into with the growth of food television. Reality cooking competitions, such as the one that had launched his career, had opened up a window on the artistry involved in creating memorable dishes while respecting the ingredients. The cameras had propelled many a chef, who might never be more than a legend in his own mind into the national spotlight.

Hunt remembered his early days in the kitchen, the harassment of his brothers, the encouragement of Mama and Alma. In the beginning he'd never given much consideration to achieving celebrity status, but the culture had changed and so had Hunt since he'd joined the ranks of James Beard Award winners. Popularity in the food world could take a chef out of the heat of the kitchen and in front of the hot lights of a film crew.

It was heady stuff for anybody, especially a boy from East Texas. And depending on where he was willing to go and how much he'd sacrifice, it could get much more intense for Hunt. He understood Jackpot's desire to live life on his own terms and in his own truck. But Jackpot also understood the rewards and benefits of corporate gigs, which were more stable with greater earning potential.

Rudy was offering that for the taking, and his wasn't the only game in town. Another call to Hunt's agent could produce any number of opportunities...as long as Hunt was willing to make the move. He'd already done Europe and the Caribbean. There was unlimited potential in Asia.

Asia? Really?

How far did he have to go to learn for himself what Cullen had said the night before?

This is home, the one place where he'd always belong. He'd do well to stick around, mend fences with old friends and let this kernel of new love have a chance to sink its roots, to blossom into something amazing. At the same time, he wasn't sure he was ready to give up advancement this early in his career and settle.

Settle? Was that any way to label the future with the dynamic woman beside him?

But to be blunt, Gillian hadn't asked him for more than a temporary commitment. She wanted his help, not the rest of his life.

There were even moments when he wasn't sure she wanted his here and now.

The future he'd been so certain of a few months ago had fled and confusion had rushed in to fill the void.

"What's on your mind?" Gillian murmured, as she glanced over her left shoulder to confirm her mother was still sleeping.

"I've been appreciating how lucky you are to know exactly what you want to do with your life."

"It's not as if you haven't figured it out for yourself."

"Well, I've found my vocation, but I'm not sure where I belong, yet."

"Belonging is a state of mind. I never imagined I'd end up in Texas, but your Pap's place called to me, so here I am. Wherever you sink roots, you eventually blossom."

Hunt did a silent double take at her use of the same metaphor that had passed through his mind moments before.

"Where'd you pick up that piece of wisdom? It sounds Texan."

"Luther was a Southerner, but I believe

he was from Georgia. He was an older gentleman I met when I was a kid. He traveled around the country pulling a small RV behind his truck, migrating with the vacationers and catching the sights himself when his shift at the hotel was done. He didn't have a lot, and while he was alone at that point in his life, he said God gave him new sights and people every day to keep him company."

"And this Luther taught you about roots and blossoming?"

"He sure did. He said life is a constant change of seasons, and even if you sink some shallow roots, you'll eventually blossom when the springtime comes along."

"And what did Luther do at the hotels?"

"He was a groundskeeper. He picked up trash and cigarette butts and dog poop, all the stuff guests leave behind expecting someone else to clean up. Luther had a song and a smile for everybody, because he was in a perpetual season of spring."

"Your friend makes life sound simple, but it's not that easy."

"*Simple* and *easy* don't mean the same

thing, Hunt. It's simple to do the right thing, but it's not always easy. It was the right thing for me to buy Temple Territory, but there's been nothing easy about making my dream a reality."

Her words sunk into his heart. Once Gillian had found what she wanted, she'd set her feet on a difficult road and never looked back. He was seeking the easy route to happiness without being certain where he was headed. First he had to figure out where he belonged and maybe the rest would seem simple.

"Has anybody reminded you lately what a smart lady you are, Gillian Moore?"

HUNT'S KIND WORDS warmed Gillian in the cool cab of the truck, but a new chill spread through her body at the suggestion she may have planted in his mind just now. She'd chosen where she wanted to be, and it was settled. Hunt had factored into her plans almost by default. But he'd only come home for a respite; he hadn't intended to stay permanently. Her purchase of Temple Territory had thrown him for an unexpected loop. But he'd gone along with her, even shown her how to shift positive momentum into high gear. Naturally she wanted his support to continue, but was it right for her to encourage a talented chef with such a limitless future to make a life-changing decision based on what was best for her?

"Smart will only get you so far if you don't use common sense," she responded to his compliment. "You've given me a heaping dose of that lesson in recent weeks, and now it's my turn to do the same." She reached across the space between them and laid her hand on his forearm.

He shrunk his chin defensively close to his chest like a turtle pulling into its shell. "I'm not sure I care for the sound of this."

"Oh, stop it." She squeezed his arm, appreciating the hard muscles beneath his shirtsleeve. "It won't hurt."

"Much?"

"Maybe a little, but that depends on you."

"Let's hear it."

"If you'd asked me yesterday for my opinion of your job offer, I'd have done everything possible to convince you to stay in Kilgore. But today I realize you should make a decision based entirely on what's best for you, Hunt. My future is literally set in stone in the form of that big cream-colored mansion. Yours is fluid, and that's as it should be. Exciting changes are taking place in the food industry, and you should be free to take advantage of whatever develops."

"Are you trying to get rid of me?" he teased, but there was concern in his tone.

Her grip on Hunt's arm increased for silent emphasis.

"We both know that's not true." Her voice was soft, not wanting her mother to overhear. "We're also well aware that I prefer to call the shots, but this one is out of my control. You're welcome to stay at Moore House for as long as you're happy, but everybody understands the better-offer principle. You're capable of a much bigger deal than I can give you, and I'll do my best to accept it when you decide it's right for you to move on to the next challenge."

Her mother began to stir, so Gillian gave

Hunt's arm one last squeeze and tucked her hand in the pouch of her hooded sweatshirt. There, she'd said what had to be said. It wasn't her place to pressure him into staying in East Texas, and that wouldn't work anyway. She had to get on with her plans and focus her energy on the multitude of tasks that had to be accomplished in a few weeks.

Hopefully the work of today would crowd out the sadness of tomorrow.

Hopefully.

THE PAGES OF the calendar flew off with the force of a Gulf Coast hurricane wind. Holiday lights went up all over town, and Hunt made good on his promise to get a star on the top of the oil derrick that stood sentry over the entrance to the mansion. The Thanksgiving parade, complete with the Kilgore Rangerettes, marched through town on the day Gillian opened her doors for the world to catch a first glimpse of Moore House.

Under Hunt's creative leadership and Alma's meticulous attention to details, the kitchen staff laid out a buffet for visiting press and local dignitaries that would make any hotelier proud. The setting was one Gillian had imagined for as long as she could remember. But as recently as yesterday she'd figured they'd never pull it together.

"This wouldn't have happened without you two." Gillian thanked her parents for the tenth time that day, but it didn't scratch the surface of her gratitude. "If you hadn't arrived when you did, it might have taken me months longer, if ever, to get to this point."

The three of them had taken their plates to the outdoor terrace where tall heaters cast halos of warmth on the tables set with linens and silver for the invited guests.

"We often encounter surprising twists on the road to our future, and very often it takes us in a different direction than what we expected," her father reminded her. "Being forced to take early retirement came as a professional blow, but in the end it was a personal blessing."

Gillian had argued with her father on

a hundred points since his arrival, but on this he was correct. It had been a blessing indeed.

"And perfectly timed," her mother added as a passing waiter offered them a cranberry mimosa.

"Did I hear the mention of perfect timing?" Hunt accepted a flute of the festive drink and took the empty seat at their table. His face glowed with satisfaction over their efforts.

"And your timing is as excellent as your taste," Gillian complimented her executive chef. She closed her eyes to savor a bite of Hunt's miso poached salmon, shook her head in wonder and smiled. "I have no idea how you do this, and I don't even want to as long as you keep doing it."

"Believe it or not the poaching broth is Alma's secret recipe, so it'll be here long after I'm gone."

"So, you've decided to take the job managing the restaurant in Austin?" James asked.

Gillian's stomach plummeted at her father's mention of the opportunity Hunt was considering. She wasn't even aware her father was in the loop on that information. Hunt had probably spoken man-to-man with her father, since he'd mentioned it so matter-of-factly.

She set down her fork, hoping her appetite for the extraordinary food would return when the conversation took a different direction.

"It's not even close to a done deal, but we're negotiating."

"Are you holding out for more money?"

"Dad! That's a rude question."

Fortunately, Hunt laughed instead of taking offense.

"I don't mind him asking." He smiled at Gillian's mortification, then answered her father. "Actually, the money's fine, but my creative freedom will be a bit hog-tied. The fact is, the restaurant is an established steak house, and the owner doesn't want to veer too far from a menu that's been quite successful. That can get old for a chef after a while, and I don't want to commit to something that might be boring in six months."

"But why would anybody court you for

your experience and reputation, and then not capitalize on those assets? That's the same as buying an expensive pair of cowboy boots and leaving them in the box," her father mused. He'd begun to work all things Texan into his speech.

"They want to put the fancy new boots on display, just not let anybody wear them," Hunt explained.

"Well, there wouldn't be any such nonsense if you stayed at Moore House," Gillian's mother insisted.

"There will be limits anywhere I work, even here. For instance the boss lady here will let me prepare fine cuisine to my heart's content, but she might object to all-you-can-eat taco night."

"If those tacos are filled with European perch or Welsh lamb, I might not object at all. I simply don't want to offer food that can be had for a fraction of the price at the local drive-through."

"We are in complete agreement." Hunt handed Gillian a fresh fork and nodded for her to give some attention to her abandoned plate.

Yes, they were in agreement on so many subjects that Gillian was hopeful there might be a future for them together. If not now, then someday.

But they didn't agree on all subjects. Aware of how strongly he'd object to the demolition and construction in the next phase, she'd intentionally withheld the information and blueprints from Hunt. Now with the first phase so close to completion and her father on board to ramrod the new project through while she and her mother ran the day-to-day operation of Moore House, the writing was on the wall, they had to move forward.

That meant applying for new permits, and once those became part of public record, it would be difficult to keep phase two under wraps.

She'd begun to view Hunt's possible move as a sign of providence. If he wasn't there to take issue and find fault in her plan, she could proceed. But if he stayed on, she'd be inclined to make changes based on his vision and never get exactly what she wanted.

Either way she'd lose something precious that she might never have again.

CHAPTER FIFTEEN

"Is there any chance you were informed and simply neglected to share the news that your wedding couple would be paying us a visit at noon today?" Hunt wheezed, winded after the sprint inside from the parking lot.

"What does that mean?" Gillian's blond brows tipped together in confusion.

"It means a black stretch Hummer pulled up right beside me just now." He pointed in the direction where the limo waited. "It was all I could do not to whip out a black felt tip and ask the folks in the passenger seat to autograph the hood of my Jeep."

The long-legged model and spike-haired rocker were as stunning in person as they were in the tabloids since they had first appeared together two decades ago.

"And you just ran in here and left them

alone?" Gillian's voice crescendoed as she prepared to take off toward the terrace.

"Of course not." Hunt grabbed her arm. He had hightailed it out of there but not before spotting James heading toward the limo, very official and in control. "Your dad and their driver are giving them the royal treatment."

"What are they doing here?" Gillian ran her hands through her hair and then down the front of her red cable-knit sweater, checking to make sure it was pulled below the hipline of her slim-fitting jeans.

"Maybe it's a trial run. Moore House is still a work in progress. You don't even have the new sign out front yet, and they've taken you at your word that you'll give them the wedding of a lifetime. Can you blame them for showing up without notice?"

"You're right, Hunt. I should have invited them down so there was no reason for this reconnaissance mission."

"Sweetie?" Meredith called from the staircase. Her furry dark shadow was on a leash by her side. "I see we have guests, and even with *my* dismal knowledge of pop culture, I'd recognize those two anywhere. That pair of no-neck monsters are probably their bodyguards."

"No-neck monsters?" Hunt questioned.

"Cat on a Hot Tin Roof? Tennessee Williams?"

He shook his head.

"I really am a pop culture dinosaur."

Hunt patted Meredith on the shoulder. "You're in good company. If a celebrity hasn't been featured on the Food Network, I'm not likely to know who they are, either. Now, let's make the best of this surprise and show our guests some Southern hospitality."

"I'm with you, Hunt. They came all the way from New York City, so let's give them their money's worth." Gillian rose to the occasion. "Mom, you're the expert on the layout and character of each suite, so I'll trust you to give the tour upstairs."

"I'm on it," she assured her daughter, as

she stroked Cooper's soft head to reward his quiet restraint.

"I'll do the honors on the main floor, and I'm sure Dad's out there right now sharing everything he's learned about the property and probably making up some more as he goes."

"I've told James all my best stories, so he'll do the history proud."

Gillian stepped closer to Hunt, seemingly not caring that her mother was watching. For a moment he expected her to lean against him for a hug of reassurance, but instead she took his hand in both of hers, as eyes the color of winter pansies met his.

"You know those cooking shows where the contestants are challenged to prepare dishes with mystery ingredients in a short amount of time?"

"I sure do. Some of my best friends are the stars on those shows."

"Well, here's your challenge. My guess is they took a private plane into East Texas Regional Airport and then caught that limo straight here. So they haven't had anything to eat. See what delectable morsels you can whip up in forty-five minutes."

"You got it," he agreed, excited to be part of Gillian's plan.

"And would you call Cullen and ask if he can get over here to be our server?"

"Great idea." His brother Cullen might be Forrest Gump when it came to setting a table, but he was Will Rogers when storytelling was in order. Hunt pulled his cell from his pocket and headed for the kitchen to raid the cooler.

GILLIAN'S KNEES WERE a little less weak than they had been moments ago. She'd always been certain she could count on her folks, and Hunt had proven time and again that he belonged on the short list of people in her corner. Very soon she'd find out if she could also number Hunt's twin among the few who would be dependable in the clutch.

"And this is the proprietor of Moore House, Miss Gillian Moore," her father was saying.

The former swimsuit model, numbered

by *People* magazine as one of the year's ten most beautiful women, was walking with her hand outstretched, a smile on her famous face.

"We've heard such good things about you from your events booking agent," the beauty enthused in her Australian-by-way-of-N.Y.C. accent. She took Gillian's hand and pulled her just close enough for an air kiss. "I hope you don't mind that we've dropped by unannounced. I realize it's rude, but we were on the way to L.A., and I couldn't resist stopping for a short while to catch a glimpse of our wedding site."

"Since nobody was expecting us, I had to agree that we just might get away with it." The raspy voice of the sixtysomething English rocker took Gillian's breath away. Was it possible that these two members of red-carpet royalty were standing at the threshold to her humble little boutique hotel?

"We can't stay long, so would you mind if we get a tour, Miss Moore?"

"Of course!" Gillian pushed past her

shock and put on her most professional smile. "And please, call me Gillian."

"And you can call me Rachel," the famous beauty offered. "Of course the whole world calls that rascal Buzz, so please feel free to do the same yourselves."

Rachel gestured toward Buzz, but he'd already wandered toward the bar where Gillian's father, bless his heart, was dropping ice cubes into a cocktail shaker.

Rachel shrugged. "Well, now that the old goat is occupied, why don't we have a look 'round? I'm mostly interested in the suites. The wedding will be shock enough for our guests. Don't want any surprises with the accommodations."

The men took their post at the bar that Mason Dixon Temple had reportedly won in a poker game in an old saloon in the Texas Hill Country. Upstairs the ladies enthused over antique armoires and vintage curtains in the lavishly appointed guest suites. Conversation among the women centered around stories of world travels and the difficulty of finding the privacy that Moore House offered.

"It's perfect!" Rachel enthused to her fiancé when they returned. She rubbed her hands, excited over the secretive plan. "Our friends will never suspect a wedding ceremony is about to take place when our charter to the West Coast has to make an *emergency* stop in Texas, of all places."

"That's because you've called it off on at least a dozen occasions, and even your own mum says you'll never go through with it."

"Don't be cheeky. Just see that you behave yourself between now and then." She lifted the olive garnish from the rim of his glass and popped it into her mouth.

"You do the same." He swatted playfully on her backside. "Our kids want me to make an honest woman out of you before they give us grandchildren."

"What is that amazing aroma?" Rachel's attention shifted as the scent of roasted garlic wafted into the room.

"I asked Chef to whip up an impromptu

luncheon for us. The dining room is all set, if you can stay a bit longer."

"I own the bloody plane," the Brit announced in his thick London accent. "And it's goin' nowhere without me."

Gillian motioned for her parents to lead the way. Rachel took Buzz by the arm and followed close behind. Gillian fell into step with her guests, hoping against hope that Hunt had pulled off something spectacular.

The gentlemen seated the ladies at a table already set with a pear salad and, on the side, a cheesy biscuit brushed with melted butter. Rachel broke off a piece of the fluffy delight and popped it into her mouth.

"Mmm, so this is the garlic I was smelling. Heavenly."

"If you're a fan of garlic, you're in for a treat, since there's more to come."

Heads turned toward the source of the comment as Cullen entered the dining room. He wore his usual ratty jeans and boots in need of polish. But over his flannel shirt he'd buttoned up one of Hunt's starched white chef coats, which lent him an official air. He smiled at Gillian, gave her a conspiratorial wink, and stopped just short of a pirouette so she could fully appreciate his attire.

"Please enjoy," he instructed, repeating what he'd heard Hunt say hundreds of times, as he placed a basket containing more biscuits in the center of their table.

Rachel's eyes widened as she stared up at Cullen.

"You're him," she gestured with her biscuit. "The Cowboy Chef! And you're every bit as spectacular in person as you are on those cooking shows," she gushed, a cross between a giddy girl and a cat on the prowl.

The woman was mistaken, of course. Cullen was a dead ringer for his twin, though anyone who saw them side by side would spot the differences in a moment, but Rachel wasn't wise to the situation.

"Thank you, ma'am," Cullen accepted the compliment without correcting her. "Life in the kitchen is hard on a man, but

I do what I can to keep the eye candy in good shape."

"Very funny," Hunt drawled as he appeared beside Cullen. "Please forgive this moron. He doesn't get out much."

"A man with an IQ of 110 hardly deserves such an insult, even from his brother."

"Isn't there an old saying about the fine line between genius and insanity?"

"Now, that's different, and under those terms, I may well qualify."

"May I introduce our executive chef, Hunt Temple, and his brother Cullen," Gillian interrupted the brotherly banter. "Cullen graciously agreed to help out on the fly today." She mouthed a sincere *thank you*.

Rachel was busy staring from one to the other, her biscuit forgotten for the moment, clearly smitten with the handsome pair.

"Have you gentlemen ever considered modeling?"

They reacted in twin fashion with the double snort Gillian had come to expect from the two. "That would cause too many technical difficulties, ma'am," Hunt drawled.

"How's that?" Rachel asked.

"When I get a guest spot on a cooking show, I'm lucky to walk past a TV camera without tripping over a cable or my own feet. This ugly goon here—" Hunt elbowed his brother "—would shatter a lens."

"I'm quite serious. The two of you would be a huge hit in Milan and Paris."

"Extraordinary cities," Cullen agreed.

"Have you been there for fashion week?"

"No, for sabbatical. I always seem to require a break right before defending a dissertation."

"Pardon me?"

"His brain is so big that he has to rest it before each PhD. It's the same with his ego." Hunt tugged at the sleeves of Cullen's chef's jacket where he'd rolled the cuffs up to expose red flannel shirtsleeves.

"Excuse these two, Rachel. This goes on constantly. They couldn't make it in modeling, because they never give the chatter a rest."

"Wait till you meet our older brothers. We're just the warm-up act," Cullen joked.

"How many of you are there?" Rachel continued to gaze back and forth, as if finding their likeness difficult to believe.

"Four."

"Are they as handsome as the two of you—and are any of you single?"

"Not quite, and yes, ma'am," Cullen confirmed.

Rachel bestowed her cover-girl smile on Gillian. "I certainly hope you'll invite them to the reception. We'll have some un-attached women in our party, and I'm sure they'd love to meet some real Texas cowboys."

"These two are going to be real dead cowboys if they don't get into the kitchen," Alma announced. She was doing her best to remain out of sight of the guests as she peeked around the corner. "Forgive me for interrupting, Señorita Gillian, but if you want the meal served while it's still hot, I need some help and *pronto.*"

Cullen glanced to the heavens for help

but then hurried from the room to do as he was instructed. Gillian's heart surged with love at the way the Temple men respected and responded to their surrogate mother.

"I can't imagine what ever made me believe being executive chef meant I was in charge," Hunt grumbled.

"Hey, you're the one who insisted on Alma being part of your deal," Gillian reminded him.

"That's absolutely true. That little woman is the rubber band that holds the Temple brothers together," Hunt explained to the guests. "Or cuts off our circulation, depending on the circumstances."

He bowed slightly and then excused himself in the direction Alma and Cullen had disappeared.

"I wasn't aware that Hunt Temple worked for you!" Rachel enthused.

"Seriously?" Gillian was stunned the news hadn't reached Rachel. "Didn't our booking agent say he was on staff?"

"No. She just said we were in for a gourmet feast and that there would be an extra special surprise at the end of the meal."

"Well, I expect you've just met the surprise."

"And he's quite a hot one at that."

"Hello. I'm sitting right here," Buzz reminded Rachel who patted his hand condescendingly.

"Kindly remember this the next time you and your chums are drooling over my Victoria's Secret friends. Anyway—" Rachel turned her eyes to Gillian "—I must say, from what I've experienced so far, you've done an amazing job renovating this old place. It's a manor house that's been brought into the new millennium, a romantic alliance of European country and no-nonsense Texas. My friends will adore it for a brief getaway."

Gillian processed Rachel's compliment, thrilled with the clear evidence that Moore House would stand on its own appeal. She didn't necessarily require the allure of a celebrity chef to draw high-end clientele. Maybe she really could land on her feet if

Hunt took that job. As much as it encouraged her to believe that might be true, her soul ached at the possibility.

It wasn't about who Hunt was in the professional world anymore. It was about who he was in her heart.

Cullen did a better-than-adequate job of serving a mouthwatering shepherd's pie and then clearing away the empty plates, while Rachel surreptitiously eyed his every move. Meanwhile Gillian's father entertained them all during the meal with the history of the property. She'd almost forgotten what a masterful storyteller he could be, and once again she was reminded of how thankful she was of their presence.

"May I interest everyone in something sweet to finish off your meal?" Hunt asked as he wheeled a dessert cart tableside. Cullen followed with a silver coffee service.

"Thank you, no, I have had an ample sufficiency and shall therefore not overtax my capacity," the Brit quipped.

Hunt lifted the dome from a serving

tray and tipped the contents for the guests to view.

"No room for English trifle, custard tarts or chocolate mousse?"

"Oh, yes, please." Buzz leaned forward to eye the desserts. "I'll have some of each."

"He most certainly will not." Rachel indicated he'd have the trifle and only a small serving at that. "Love, you can't keep eating as if you have a rugger match every night or you can't expect to zip up the trousers of your new tux."

"Can't imagine why I have to wear a bloody tux."

"In the first place, because I said so. And in the second place, because our wardrobes were custom-made for the occasion. We'll repay the courtesy by wearing Dolce & Gabbana in our wedding photos, or pay them the same as the rest of the world with cash from your pocket."

"Well said," he agreed, his mouth full of sherry-soaked lady fingers and whipped cream.

"Hunt, won't you join us?" Meredith suggested after everyone had been served, and Cullen had excused himself.

"I don't want to impose." Hunt dipped his chin modestly.

"Nonsense." Rachel scooted to the side to make room so that Hunt could bring another chair to the table. "Wc should talk about the wedding menu. Now that I'm aware that the Cowboy Chef is in the kitchen, it changes everything in a most delightful way."

Hunt's smoky eyes narrowed as they sought Gillian's. He'd caught the message that he hadn't been the contract-signing bonus after all. How would the news of her deception impact his decision to stay or move on?

And how would Gillian's heart deal with it either way?

CHAPTER SIXTEEN

"I'M SO GLAD you changed your mind about Mac's party," Hunt murmured near Gillian's ear as he helped her into a full-length faux fur coat.

"Once again, you were right," she admitted as she turned in his arms but stepped away, putting space between them. "As natural as it is for me to deal with strangers every day, it's outside of my comfort zone to socialize with people I haven't met."

"But you're going to be living and working with these folks, and a holiday party is the perfect way to get to know them in a festive setting where you're *not* on the job."

He'd been hounding her lately to spend a bit more time away from Moore House and becoming friendlier with the locals.

He was glad that she was trusting him, at least about some things. It still smarted that she'd deceived him about being part of the deal with Rachel and Buzz, but he understood. Moore House was important to Gillian, and she'd do whatever it took to make it a success.

"You're one to talk, Hunt Temple! Even when you're not planning for our guests, you're cooking for the staff or you're in the kitchen at Cullen's house. I'm surprised you're not preparing hors d'oeuvres at this moment."

"My brother's savvy enough to realize I deserve a break. Besides, he's got ideas of his own when it comes to catering."

"For instance?"

"Oh, you'll understand when we get out there."

"Sorry to keep you two waiting," Meredith apologized as she and James reached the bottom of the grand staircase.

Gillian got her business sense from her father and her beauty from her mother, who was particularly lovely in a sparkly black cocktail dress with lace sleeves.

"Mom, you look fabulous! I knew that Zac Posen would fit you like a glove."

"Thanks." She tugged at the hem. "You don't think it's too short for my age?"

"Showing half of your knee is not exactly risqué."

"What's underneath that coat?" Meredith eyed her daughter suspiciously.

"Don't worry, Mrs. Moore, it's already been approved," Hunt only half teased. Gillian was stunning in red satin, and he'd stick close to her side tonight to make sure the single men didn't get too friendly.

"I hope you were able to find your winter coats among your packing boxes," Hunt commented. It was a brisk night.

"They're on the rack by the terrace doors. But my coat is a dozen years old. I have to find myself a stylish new fur. Gillian's is perfection."

"Mom, your vintage lamb's wool will never go out of style," she assured her mother.

"If the fashion police are finished, can we be on our way? I'm starving," James reminded them, grumpy with hunger.

His wife unwrapped a chocolate truffle she pulled from her bag and popped it into his mouth. He smiled for the first time that day.

"Are you sure you don't want to take one car?" Hunt asked as they approached the parking lot.

"No, thanks," James answered more kindly after his sugar fix. "With Cooper in his crate, we can't stay away very long, and we don't want to make you young folks end your evening too soon."

The ride out to Lake Cherokee was quiet as they enjoyed Christmas carols on the radio, and Hunt kept an eye on the rear-view mirror.

"Thanks for inviting my parents and giving us the opportunity to meet the rest of your brothers, Hunt."

"Don't you figure it's time we all got together, since fate seems to have made us one big family already?"

"I guess I hadn't considered it that way. Once in a while I forget that I bought what might have been your inheritance, if things had gone differently years ago."

Hunt mulled over the way Gillian interpreted what he'd said. After several miles he heard a sigh escape from his lips before he realized it was coming.

"Deep down you're still angry with me, aren't you, Hunt?"

"Maybe there's some subconscious envy still at work. But angry? Definitely not." He shook his head, certain of his response.

"Then what's on your mind?"

His gut said he'd either be a fool to speak up now or a bigger one to keep his feelings to himself much longer. The calendar was against him no matter how this evening played out.

"Gillian, when I mentioned fate just now, Temple Territory wasn't even on my mind."

She twisted in her seat to catch his face in the light from the Jeep's dashboard. Hers was so lovely it stole his breath. With the faux fox collar tucked up around her neck, she resembled a princess about to take a winter sleigh ride.

"Then what were you referring to?"

"Us."

"What about us, Hunt?"

She was quiet as he weighed his words carefully.

"Gillian." Hunt reached across the center console and took her gloved hand. "I care about you a great deal."

"But?"

"But nothing. At the risk of aggravating you at the beginning of our date, I want to state again that making the most of our time together is what's important to me."

She slipped her hand from his and tucked it into the pocket of her coat.

"That should be enough, Hunt. But it's not. I have so much work ahead of me to make the hotel successful. Once the wedding has come and gone, any press coverage we get out of it will be forgotten in a week. I've got to focus on promoting Moore House instead of worrying over when you're going to announce your departure. And I don't want to grieve your loss once you've moved on. The only way to prevent that worry and grief is to simply not go down that road."

"But I thought you weren't ready for anything permanent, either?"

"I'm not."

"Well, if you don't want anything long-term and you won't seize the day, then I guess that totally leaves me without options."

His gut had been right. He felt like a fool.

GILLIAN BIT HER tongue and held back the words that would clear this all up or blow it wide open. She was playing semantics with Hunt. Being ready for a permanent relationship and wanting one were entirely different. She might never be ready, because there was so much that she was determined to accomplish in her career.

In her heart of hearts she desperately wanted to accept whatever Hunt could offer. But didn't she deserve more than being an *option* with him? Didn't she deserve the forever that both sets of their parents had found with one another? Maybe Hunt had lost that exposure to his folks' love so young that he'd forgotten what it looked like, but she hadn't.

She glanced at the side mirror and the car following close behind on the dark road. She could see her mother leaning as near to her father as the seat belts would allow. They were probably holding hands and sharing quiet conversation.

Yes, there was another *option,* but it involved the kind of forever commitment that Hunt was unlikely to offer and maybe even incapable of making.

He slowed the Jeep, rounded a dark curve and the holiday party underway at McCarthy's house blazed into view up ahead. The pines shimmered with thousands of colored twinkle lights, and the tall outline of a Christmas tree at the water's edge reflected off the surface of the lake.

Gillian had to get back into the festive mood that her parents and their hosts were expecting.

"Hunt, we knew from the very first day that our time together was limited, and we each accepted the other's ground rules. But that hasn't stopped us from accomplishing more than I ever imagined we would together. So let's celebrate by enjoying where we are in life at the moment. Can we do that?"

Hunt followed the signals of the young men directing traffic, found a spot for two vehicles and eased to the side of the road. He switched off the engine and looked toward her with an easy smile.

"Of course. Forgive me for almost spoiling our evening."

He hurried around to the passenger's side of the Jeep, helped her out and continued to hold her close against the cold wind rising off the water.

"This place is incredible!" her father called. "Remind us again what McCarthy does for a living?"

"He's only a bean counter."

"Yes, and you're only a cook." James actually laughed.

"How about the other two?" Meredith asked.

"Cullen's a professional teacher's pet, and Joiner's a cowboy wannabe."

"You sure do make light of your family's successes," James commented.

"We're all that way. The Temple brothers are okay with where we are in life at the moment. As your daughter recently reminded me, that's not a bad policy."

Gillian expected those last words were

meant to make her reconsider her suggestion, but maybe she'd wisely set them on a new course. Whether it was the right one or not would be revealed in the weeks ahead.

"A LUAU?" GILLIAN WAS caught off guard by the theme as she surveyed the Hawaiian decor inside McCarthy's home. She offered up her coat to be hung on a nearby rack in case she decided to take a stroll to the lake.

"Sure!" Hunt enthused, tongue in cheek. "Who doesn't love a good pig roast in thirty-five-degree weather? A luau shouts 'Ho! Ho! Ho!' if you ask me."

Through the expanse of windows she could see dozens of guests enjoying the clear, cold night on the waterfront lawn. They hovered for warmth and conversation around a huge stone fire pit or one of several cauldron-style pits. When the patio door opened, a mouthwatering aroma drifted inside, and Gillian couldn't wait to sample whatever was on that outdoor barbecue. Colorfully dressed waiters offered coconut fried shrimp, grilled pineapple on skewers and chunks of beautiful Ahi tuna.

For the more adventurous there was Hawaiian poi and Spam sushi.

Cullen and two other men made their way through the crowded room to greet the newcomers. Introductions were unnecessary. The family resemblance made it obvious these men were Hunt's older brothers.

"Gillian, Meredith and James Moore, you've met Cullen, and these two ugly fellas are our older brothers, Joiner and McCarthy."

As they shook hands all around, Meredith asked, "Where do you gentlemen get your unique names?"

"Our daddy called us each after a successful wildcatter," Joiner explained. "It was his attempt to offset the impact of our last name. When we were all born, his Pap was in prison for stealing oil—that's the only thing in Texas worse than rustling cattle."

"Daddy never said that himself, but it makes a good story so that's the one we're stickin' with," McCarthy insisted. "So, how do you like my Hawaiian holiday, East Texas style?"

"Enough to repeat it at Moore House, but maybe in the summer by the pool."

"I can understand why that might be practical if you want hula girls and fire twirlers, but you must admit that, as a Christmas theme, this is unique."

"And quite unexpected, which is the whole idea behind the element of surprise."

"I've gotta say it takes a lot to surprise my palate, but you certainly did it with this sushi from a can." Hunt finished off his bite of grilled Spam atop a block of rice wrapped in seaweed.

"What, that's all it took? I could have saved a lot of money on that pig out there."

"Hey," Joiner chimed in. "This is Christmas, not Hunt's birthday. The rest of us want something besides mystery meat on a cracker for dinner. Porky will not have died in vain, I assure you."

A cheer went up on the lawn as the men working the fire pit lifted off the grill and transferred the main course to a pair of sawhorses set up to serve as a carving station.

"Everybody grab a plate," McCarthy encouraged his guests. "It's time for a pig pickin'!"

"I'm sorry you ladies got into designer dresses to serve yourselves, sit on folding chairs and cover your laps with paper napkins."

"Nonsense, Hunt." Meredith waved away his apology. "I love people who color outside the lines. We'll be doing a lot of that when we plan Moore House events."

"I was just thinking the same thing, Mom. We should reconsider our plans for the grand opening event. We ought to stage something that is not only unforgettable but leaves people talking about us for weeks afterward." Gillian covered her mouth and spoke where only their small circle could hear. "And I mean something unforgettable that will have folks talking about Moore House and not you-know-who and her British boyfriend."

Hunt heard excitement in Gillian's voice at the prospect of setting her hotel apart with an extraordinary surprise, and suddenly he wanted to make that happen for her. Getting more extraordinary than a rock star wedding would be quite a feat, but Hunt just might be able to pull it off.

CHAPTER SEVENTEEN

"MOM, EVERYONE WAS so kind at the party last night. Hunt's old friends even invited me to come to their Sunday afternoon baseball games in the spring, and if Hunt's in town, he's going to be their pitcher. In so many ways, living here is as if I had been dropped into Mayberry."

"That's wonderful. So why the long face?"

"Because this morning I'm feeling bad."

"About what?"

"If Buzz and Rachel's wedding goes off as we've planned, it's going to bring publicity and strangers and noise into town, and maybe not always in a good way. It'll blow the lid off their quiet lives."

"Baby girl, some of those changes have to come in order for us to make a living here."

Winter sun streamed through the new

bay window onto the table in the kitchen where Gillian and her mother enjoyed a late cup of coffee. They sat together at the oversize built-in table installed especially for the lucky few diners who would get to watch the kitchen's activity and interact with the Cowboy Chef himself. Or whoever replaced Hunt one day.

"Gillian, business is business. None of those folks who went on and on about their peaceful little town would trade paying jobs for quiet. You can throw a rock and hit any number of places where people can live undisturbed because there is no activity, no work and no income. They'll be grateful that you're stirring things up a bit."

"Still, isn't it wrong for me not to spell out the change that's less than two weeks away?"

"Gillian, if you have to spell it out, they won't get it anyway."

"I suppose you're right."

Now that her mother had mentioned it, Gillian had never heard of an employer or business owner making a big confession about how their success might impact the community, other than in a good way with more jobs. And everybody was glad to hear that news. Along with any growth there were bound to be minor aggravations such as traffic and new construction and, with any luck, media.

"Do I at least owe it to Hunt to show him the plans for phase two? He's going to hit the roof."

"Gillian, that's entirely up to you. But you're the property owner, not Hunt. It's your job to make decisions that are best for your hotel, and you don't require Hunt's approval or his support. I realize you two have feelings for one another, but they're not set in stone."

"They're not even set in number two pencil."

"Exactly." Her mother folded the news-paper she'd been reading and laid it be-side her coffee cup. "Let's get phase one open and running while you continue the research on the spa. When the conditions are right you'll share the plans with Hunt, and you'll find the perfect words to explain your decisions."

Forever in housekeeping mode, Meredith crossed to the deep stainless-steel sink to empty the coffeepot and dump the grounds in the compost bowl before wiping down the granite counter.

"Where are you and Dad off to today?" Gillian followed her mother's lead, soaped and rinsed her coffee cup, then placed it on the drain board.

"We're going out to Lake Cherokee—this time in the daylight—to look for rentals. A home on the water would be something entirely different for us, and Cooper would love swimming with the ducks whenever the mood strikes him. We might even get him a buddy when we have more room."

"I hadn't considered you and Dad moving out so soon." She felt the loss already. "I've enjoyed your company."

"We'd always planned to find a place of our own, and you'll want our suite for paying guests."

"There's no rush to go anywhere, Mom." Why was everyone in a hurry to be on their way out of Gillian's life?

"We'll be working here with you at least

six days a week for a while, so it's not as if we won't be close. And if I'm not mistaken, you weren't exactly thrilled when we arrived on your doorstep. You expected us to argue with you on all your decisions and pressure you to do things differently, didn't you?"

Gillian's cheeks flushed. "How did you guess?"

"Easy. We imagined how we would have felt if our parents had shown up without being invited. It wasn't hard to figure out that we were invading your space." Her mother linked an arm with Gillian's, pulling her close for a private moment.

"I realize how it is for you and your dad to be under the same roof again. You're both decisive and stubborn and controlling. But you're also hardworking and creative." She squeezed her daughter tight. "He's very proud of you. We both are."

"Mom, you and Dad have made such an incredible sacrifice for me. I'm sorry if I've done or said anything that seemed ungrateful." Gillian couldn't believe she and her mother were having this conversation. They must think they'd raised a spoiled brat.

"You haven't offended us in any way, sweetheart. You've been more than gracious to include us in everything, especially when a young man is unwittingly courting you."

Gillian's chin snapped up as if her mother had smacked her on the forehead. "What do you mean, courting me?"

"*Unwittingly* courting you."

"What makes you say such a thing?" Gillian pretended not to understand her mother's observation. The truth was she felt the same way some days...and then others Hunt would return to being her chef and nothing more.

"It's okay if you don't want to admit it, even to yourself. You care for that young man, quite a bit. You're nervous about how it's going to impact your life if he stays, and you're scared of how you'll deal with the pain if he goes."

She took her daughter's face in both hands.

"Let me clue you in, baby girl. He shares

your concerns for the same reasons. Even so, he courts you, not fully understanding what it is he's doing. I for one believe he'll figure it out before it's too late."

"What makes you so confident?"

"Things weren't so different between your father and me at your age. We played cat and mouse but we knew what we wanted. And you know, too. Just give your heart time and wait for Hunt to declare himself. Trust your mother in this. It'll be a piece of cake for him to speak his heart when the right moment comes."

"MISS GILLIAN, ARE YOU absolutely sure these are the plans you want to follow for phase two? What you're tearing down and covering over has pretty significant value to some people. Hunt's gonna have a runaway when he finds out."

"It can't be helped, Karl," Gillian explained.

Karl's crew had done such a great job that she'd contracted Hunt's old friend again to enclose the courtyard of the mansion and install a luxurious spa.

"I'm not going to have a dry-water well in the middle of my hotel just because it's supposed to have *mystical* value. That thing is dangerous, and it stinks."

"But if you'll let me get an architect on it, there might be a creative way to save it, if you know what I mean."

"Karl, I appreciate your concern. But I'm the property owner and that gives me the final word on the land, including that hole in the ground."

"Yes, ma'am, that's correct. You have the last say. But there's folklore tied to that old well, and Pap Temple intentionally built around it because he respected those tales, though they were a bit tall even by Texas standards."

"Exactly. There's no shortage of tall tales and big fish stories around here. One less pinpoint on the map for speculation won't hurt anything."

"But still, when *certain people* find out…"

"Are *you* going to be the one to break the news to *certain people* that I plan to build over that eyesore, Karl?"

"No, ma'am." He shook his head emphatically. "When I took this job, I made a commitment to you and the men on my payroll. If you want those rocks torn down and that old hole in the ground filled with cement, that's what we'll do. I just want to make sure you're aware it will wipe away sentimental as well as hocus-pocus attachments. Are you sure you don't want to talk to Hunt about this first?"

"Thanks, but no." She closed the subject with a shake of her head. Her mind was made up. "I appreciate being able to count on you, Karl. The work you've done so far has been first-rate, and that's exactly what I expect for the spa and salon. Those amenities will bring even more jobs and commerce into town. Within fifteen minutes of opening those doors, nobody will remember that well ever existed."

"Have it your way, Miss Gillian."

"Have you heard from the city on the new permits?"

"Not yet, but we put them in plenty early this go-around so we should be approved to start extending the roof by mid-January.

Your new spa should be open by the end of February."

"That sounds perfect, Karl. We have a private party planned for the weekend just before New Year's, and general reservations open up on January first. You should be able to get the work done on the new space without too much inconvenience to our guests."

"We'll keep the construction to daylight hours on weekdays, just as you and I discussed." He glanced at his wristwatch and settled his Stetson on his head. "If there's nothing else, I should be on my way."

"Karl, there is one thing." She put a hand on his forearm. "As soon as the permit is issued, I expect you to get a couple of men over here to take care of that well. Let's keep it quiet, if you know what I mean."

"Yes, ma'am. You want that well gone before anybody hears about your plans and tries to throw a monkey wrench in your works."

"That's one way to interpret it."

"I guarantee you that's how my buddy Hunt's gonna interpret it, but we've already been down that road." Karl touched the brim of his hat to show his respect and headed for his pickup.

"I'M ITCHING TO get a full crew in here so we can service a packed dining room," Hunt enthused. Gillian stood beside him at the kitchen countertop as they admired the hanging pot rack he'd just installed.

Even though there were no meals to prepare, he'd come over daily to arrange his supplies in just the proper place, tweaking his setup as he became familiar with the storage bins in the prep stations. He also preferred to interview and meet with the staff in close quarters to get a feel for how they'd interact in his kitchen.

His kitchen. There it was again. He had to keep reminding himself it wasn't his kitchen.

"Isn't it driving you nuts to see your suites upstairs sitting empty?" He focused on Gillian to get his mind off selfish thoughts.

"It sure is, but that was part of the contract we signed with Rachel and Buzz. It's important to them to be the first to rent the entire estate so there's absolutely no chance they'll be accused of ripping off what someone else has already done."

"Isn't it amazing and sorta sad how people with that kind of money have to plot and scheme their every move?"

"Oh, it is, Hunt. It truly is." Gillian's voice was flooded with exaggerated compassion. "It depresses me so much I can hardly sleep at night. I toss and turn over my concern that poor Rachel can easily afford to rent my place for weeks just to one-up her neighbors."

Hunt examined Gillian closely to see if she was making fun of him. But when she spewed out laughter, he couldn't help but join her. It was a silly moment they both needed, and they fell against one another, elbows on the granite counter, laughing until their sides hurt. Gillian stopped to catch her breath and rub the tears from the outer corners of her eyes. Her silky blond hair was caught up in a stretchy thing, and her ponytail bobbed above the round neck of a chocolate-colored sweater. He brushed two fingers across her forehead where her bangs had settled on damp, dark lashes.

"You were stunning in that red satin at Mac's, but today you are even more beautiful."

The amusement that had been on her face slipped away, a serious expression replacing the smile. "That's a very kind thing for you to say, Hunt."

He slid his hand across the smooth skin at her nape, lightly cupped her neck and pulled her face close to his own.

"It wasn't meant to be kind."

"Then what was it meant to be?" she asked, her full lips so very close.

"A compliment for…" The words stuck in his throat.

"…for the boss lady?" Gillian tried to spoil the moment, but he wasn't going to let that happen.

"For the woman who has captured my heart."

He realized with a start that *capture* was exactly the right word. So that's what Hunt did to Gillian's mouth before she had the chance to get logical on him and pull away.

He held one hand at her neck and smoothed the other down her spine to settle at her waist, then he pulled her close to his chest. Hunt couldn't get enough of the softness of her skin and the sound of her sighs matching his own. This nearness, this oneness with a woman he loved was a sensation he'd never dared to imagine. He was getting a glimpse into what his married friends meant when they talked about wanting to be with one person for the rest of their lives.

The rest of their lives?

Hunt dragged his lips from Gillian's, settled a soft kiss at her temple and held her quietly while he waited for the thumping of his heart to slow.

The rest of their lives?

It was a sobering consideration for the Cowboy Chef who enjoyed his gallivanting lifestyle and unsettled ways. He'd always been decisive about his career, and where he wanted to hone and practice his skills.

But how could he give up his freedom

and his future for the sake of a dream that was Gillian's? How could he not?

"Hunt, I don't believe we're ready to have this conversation," she whispered against his chest.

Not letting either of them dwell on the emotional moment, he broke the silence. "You're right, and I have an idea."

It was up to him to to get them both out of this very private environment before they said and did things they might regret.

"Your folks were smart to take advantage of this beautiful day and an empty hotel to get out and have some fun. Let's drive over to Longview and shop for Christmas gifts. There are only a few days left, and there's not a single real gift beneath your tree."

They'd decorated a huge spruce in the entry for the press event but the colorfully wrapped boxes were empty, all for show.

"I'd love to do some shopping! I want to get something special for my folks to thank them for their help. Do you exchange gifts with your brothers?"

"We do, but our presents for each other always seem to have stupid jokes associated with them. Not so with our gifts for Alma and Felix, though. There's a pretty stiff competition in that category."

"Well, since your brothers don't have the help of a lifelong female shopper, I can safely say you'll win the gift wars this year. Let me grab my coat."

He watched Gillian leave the room, and as she put even that brief distance between the two of them, he began to ache for her return.

Yes siree, Bob. The Cowboy Chef's unattached status is in a heap of trouble.

CHAPTER EIGHTEEN

THE MALL WAS packed with holiday shoppers, so Hunt opted for a string of independently owned boutiques instead. He offered to drop Gillian at the sidewalk, but she insisted on traipsing through the maze of parked cars with him. He took her hand and tugged her close as they crossed a busy street. She returned the tight squeeze of his hand and gave him a wink, leaving Hunt to wonder whether it was his touch or Christmas bargains that had her grinning with excitement.

"I hear these shops carry merchandise so trendy that you can't even find them at the big retail stores. We should be able to get something great for Alma and maybe even some one-of-a-kind gift items for our spa shop."

"But why would you buy merchandise

now when you're not going to start the construction on your spa for months?"

For some reason, Gillian was caught off guard by the question, and she stumbled.

She pitched forward and landed hard on one knee. Hunt was glad he'd had a firm hold on her left hand or else she might have gone down face-first into the brick pavers. He squatted close to check her for injuries while she glanced about.

"Please tell me nobody saw that," she begged.

"No such luck," he teased to cover his concern. "But you were smart to fall among the Audis and Jags, so only a few extremely wealthy shoppers would spot your fall. Way to minimize your embarrassment."

"Help me up." She swatted away his hands as he tried to straighten her leg. "I must look like a fool down here."

"Why don't you sit still for a minute and let me call an ambulance?"

"An ambulance?" Gillian squeaked. "You can't be serious. I just want to get up and walk it off."

But when she tried to push to her feet,

the injured knee collapsed beneath her. He was sure she'd have bit through her lip before she cried, but Gillian's grimace assured him the pain was severe.

"You're obviously not going to simply walk this off. If you won't let me call an ambulance, will you at least let me carry you back to the Jeep?"

As he wrapped her in his arms, her lovely eyes flew wide and alarm creased the smooth skin between her brows.

"What? Are you opposed to somebody mistaking me carrying you in my arms for a public display of affection?"

"No, I'm opposed to missing our shopping trip." She pouted, and Hunt sunk more deeply in love with her.

"Now I'm *sure* you're not badly hurt." He scooped Gillian close and held her tightly as he stood. "But just to be safe we're going to make a stop by the medical center for an X-ray of that knee. They'll give you something for the pain."

"Hunt, it's Saturday. We'll have to wait for hours."

"Maybe not. Daddy was chief of surgery

when our parents were killed. It was a lot of years ago, but my brothers and I still get treated like family by the medical staff. I'll be shocked if there isn't at least one person in there who calls me Doc Temple's youngest boy and not the Cowboy Chef."

HER KNEE WAS throbbing so badly that Gillian had lost any inclination to argue against going to the E.R. At this point she was just silently hoping there were no ligament tears or bone breaks. And to add insult to injury, the fall had been entirely her fault.

She'd stumbled at Hunt's mention of the time line for building the spa. At least he was none the wiser as to the reason for her clumsy reaction. *Guilty reaction,* to be truthful. She couldn't help feeling that she was betraying him by keeping her plans from him. But she'd confess everything once the well was gone, and it wouldn't be the big deal Karl expected.

Hunt would be okay with it.

Yeah, right.

The woman in the E.R. admissions of-

fice greeted Hunt with a motherly hug.
Gillian was wheeled toward the X-ray department within the hour. And within another hour she'd been discharged with her
leg in a gosh-awful gray knee brace and a
pair of crutches.

"This is not exactly the *pop of color* I
was hoping to pair with my secondhand
Jimmy Choo pumps on New Year's Eve."

"Just be thankful your knee is encased
in Velcro and not plaster." Hunt lifted Gillian, settled her into the Wrangler's passenger's seat and handed the safety belt across
her lap.

"Oh, I am," she insisted as she tightened
the belt. "From what the orthopedic surgeon said, it could have been much worse,
so it's minor in the big picture. Still, this
is a setback I could do without. How am I
ever going to manage?"

Hunt climbed behind the wheel and
waved away her melodrama. "That brace
may slow you down a bit, but that's probably a good thing."

"How can you say that? You know who's
about to descend on Kilgore and how much

is at stake. Everything's got to go perfectly, and I can't imagine how that's going to happen with me in this straitjacket."

There were a myriad of decorative displays and personal touches still to be added to the hotel. At least three pages in her notebook were filled with important bullet points still to be checked off, and a call with Rachel was scheduled for Monday to discuss the ceremony.

"You've been reminding me all morning how much help your parents have been. They'll stand in wherever they have to, and I'm available to do the same. Between us and the staff we've hired, all the details will get covered, and the wedding will go off without a hitch. As soon as we get you home, you can start making each of us a list of chores, and we'll get right on them."

"I suppose you're right." Though her brain was already foggy from pain medication, she began to churn through a mental to-do list. "There are thousands of white lights that have to be strung about the grounds and hung from the trees, the perfect project for Dad and Felix. Mom will be happy to help Alma with the petit fours we'd planned to bake and freeze."

She leveled a sheepish look his way.

"What?"

"I've been meaning to ask if you'd take over the menu discussions with Rachel. I wanted to keep my hand in it, but that's your bailiwick. I should probably get out of the way and let a professional finish the job. Would you mind?"

"Of course I wouldn't mind." He sounded relieved, as if he'd feared she'd never come to that conclusion.

"I've already shared my notes with you, but she's supposed to call on Monday, and I'm not sure how much good I'll be once the drugs kick in."

"No problem. I'll take the call on speakerphone so you can hear the whole thing and still be informed. You won't have any issues directing those projects from your rooms on the second floor for a few days," he assured her.

"Thank goodness for the elevator or I'd have to move into the laundry room downstairs."

"Cullen's also got two more guest rooms at his place. I'm sure we could relocate some boxes of books to make a comfortable spot for you, if necessary."

She reached across the space between them to rest her hand on his shoulder and was reminded once again that the man beneath the jacket was solid, dependable and oh-so masculine.

"You've been too good to me, Hunt. How can I show my appreciation?"

"You've already shown me in a dozen ways." He put his left palm atop her hand and gave it a firm squeeze before placing it back on the steering wheel.

"Really?" She exaggerated the one-word question. "How so?"

He smiled, his eyes wide in amusement at her shameless request for an attagirl.

"Not that I'm fishing for kudos," she feigned innocence.

"Neither of us ever would." He returned her insistence with a shake of his head. "Well, let me see. First there's the way you've brought Alma and Felix into your business, and then how you've treated my brothers as if they're old friends. Next there's the fact that you've given me complete control of the kitchen and my own staff."

She was surprised by that last comment. "Didn't you expect that I'd do that, Hunt?"

"Not at first, no. You were pretty adamant about calling all the shots, but then most owners are, even when they hire an accomplished chef to run the show. I figured for sure we'd knock heads a lot during the build out, but you surprised me."

"I'm glad to hear that, Hunt. But it was you who showed me I had to take a step away and let my experts do the job I'd hired them to do. Otherwise I might have been in this knee brace even sooner."

"Or handcuffs," he teased. "I was afraid the city permit office might sic the law on you, after the way you harassed them. You're lucky Mac was able to get his commissioner buddy to smooth things over with them."

"That was a valuable lesson in small-town living. Don't go scratching in somebody else's sandbox, and if you do, be sure you have a friend with a shovel at City Hall."

She shook her head at her own stubbornness. He'd been right to tell her to ease off, and she'd been foolish not to follow his guidance.

"But, Gillian, the most important way you've shown your appreciation was by being open-minded about the history of Temple Territory. You've kept the most well-known points of interest in place, and not only is that important to the integrity of the property, it's important to my family."

He turned into the winding drive and drove up the hill to the empty parking lot at the rear of the mansion.

Gillian chose her words carefully, shifting in her seat. "Hunt, I haven't agreed with you on all those *points of interest*. But when something makes sense, adds to the allure of the hotel and doesn't stray too far from my vision, I've tried to be flexible. Just look how well your Pap's saloon bar cleaned up."

"I couldn't believe you had that scarred

piece of junk refinished, and moved front and center."

"That piece of junk is a fabulous example of Western Americana, and I recognized its value the moment I laid eyes on it out in the barn. If there hadn't already been a good story to go with it, I'd have made one up!"

"I doubt that Pap had many reasons for pride in the last years of his life. That beat-up old bar being transformed into a focal point for your hotel would make him very proud indeed." Hunt nodded with a smile. "You warm my heart every time you rescue something of his, so don't feel as if you have to do anything special to make the message official."

Gillian silently hoped that what she had up her sleeve would be enough to honor the old man who'd once called this place his home, and enough to make up for her deception. She was not a rule breaker. She'd lived her life asking permission in advance, but in this case, she'd have to ask for forgiveness after the fact.

"Now that I've got this bum knee, how

will I thank my parents? There won't be any holiday gift shopping for me."

"You can always order something off the internet or from one of those cable shopping networks. There's still time for UPS to get it here."

"That's an option. But they deserve more than the cheesecake-of-the-month club."

"We'll worry about gifts tomorrow. For now let's get you upstairs to your rooms, where we can elevate and ice that knee."

"You don't have to go to all that trouble. If you'll dump me in the lobby, I'll be fine until Mom and Dad get home from the lake."

"Just leave everything to me," he insisted.

Hunt scooped her out of the seat and carried her inside. He continued past the sofa she pointed to, easily mounted the staircase worthy of Scarlett O'Hara's Atlanta home, and lowered Gillian onto the chaise longue in her sitting room. He put a pillow beneath her knees, grabbed the Sherpa throw from the foot of the four-poster bed and draped it over her lap.

"I'll be up in a few minutes," he called from the door. She counted as his boots thumped down twenty-four steps and then fell silent, as he probably crossed the mesquite floor in the direction of the kitchen that was his domain.

The spirit of Hunt Temple would forever be etched on her property and her heart. And she wanted it to remain that way. It was right. It was fitting. It was perfect.

It was love.

"Oh, my goodness," Gillian muttered to herself, daring to say the words out loud.

"I love him," she whispered. Tears stung her eyes. "I love Hunt."

She pressed her fingertips to her lips as if to stop any further leaks of the admission that could never be recalled. Gillian shuddered over the revelation, even though it was a truth she'd known for weeks but had refused to recognize.

She loved Hunt Temple.

But the timing was all wrong. The throbbing in her head began to match the throbbing in her knee. Gillian leaned her forehead against the heels of both hands and closed her eyes. Nothing serious with Hunt could work out.

They were star-crossed, doomed from the get-go. Weren't they?

She and Hunt wanted different things. She considered how often he'd paralleled their roles in the hospitality industry, the reasons why they were well matched, if only for the short term.

Well, maybe they shared a passion for serving guests, but at this point, the logistics of their relationship were unstable at best. Her home was here in Kilgore, and would be for many years to come if she was blessed with success. As Hunt had proven over and over, his employment and his home could be anywhere. His talent was mobile and in demand. He had traveled half the world and didn't seem inclined to settle for this small East Texas town again.

But Kilgore was Hunt's home.

His family and friends were here. His roots were here. He always came back. Didn't that mean this was where his heart wanted to be?

Hope surged past the emotional roadblocks Gillian was putting up as fast as she could. Maybe there was a chance for the two of them to be together. Maybe.

Gillian laid her head against the chaise, closed her eyes and let the medication do its work.

"How'd the house hunting go?" Hunt asked James and Meredith when they arrived at Moore House just before sunset.

"We found several rentals that we can afford, and Cooper was in hog heaven," James reported.

The big poodle raced gracefully from room to room on the main floor, as if he were running the bases in a ball park. The dog's ability to turn on a dime without disturbing his surroundings was amazing. He definitely deserved a space to call his own, and the inside of a manor house was not the ideal location.

Even so, being around Cooper made Hunt want a big dog of his own. But a big dog meant a big yard. Big yard meant big house. Big house meant big mortgage, and big mortgage naturally made Hunt consider

Temple Territory and the commitment he'd shied away from all of his adult life.

If he were honest, it didn't bother him nearly as much as it once had to think of this place as Gillian's. Hunt wasn't just whistling Dixie when he'd told Gillian her gestures to maintain the history of the property honored his family, and day by day he realized that was enough.

"We were able to reach the Realtor, and she agreed to meet us out there tomorrow," James continued. "She said this is traditionally a slow time for lake rentals, and we can probably lock into a year's lease at a good rate."

"Tomorrow, huh?" Hunt questioned.

"Why? What's going on?" Meredith's mama-radar shot up. She glanced around. "Where's Gillian?"

"She's going to be fine." He held both palms out to assure Gillian's parents. "She fell today when we were out shopping and banged up her knee pretty badly. We made a trip to the E.R., and she'll be on crutches for a few weeks, but the orthopedic doesn't believe she'll even require physical therapy."

"Is she upstairs?" Meredith headed for the staircase with Cooper close behind.

"Yes, ma'am. She's probably asleep by now, but if not, she may be kinda goofy from the pain meds, so don't be alarmed."

"Poor Gillian," James breathed. "This is the last thing my daughter should have to deal with right now."

"Sir, that's exactly what Gillian said, but I reassured her that, between the three of us and the staff, we'd get everything done."

"Under her close scrutiny, of course," her father added with a smile.

"Of course. She says she was mentored by the master of control."

"That would be her mother, all right."

"Sir, you do realize, when your daughter speaks of her mentor, she's talking about you, right?"

James opened his mouth and sucked in a breath as if preparing to argue. But he remained silent, mulling over what Hunt said. Could this be his first realization that he'd molded Gillian into a control freak? Or was it the thought of being his daughter's mentor that stole his words? Father and daughter were so very much alike. Between the two of them, Moore House couldn't help but be a success.

"Hunt, would you mind excusing us for the evening? I'm going to go up and check on Gillian, and then I'll take care of dinner for my girls."

"Of course, you should have some family time. Are you sure I can't prepare a meal for you?" He'd already laid out the *mise en place* for chicken piccata.

James shook his head. "You've done enough for one day, and we can't thank you enough for getting her to the E.R. I'll make us some grilled cheese sandwiches and open a can of tomato soup. That's the only thing Gillian would eat as a child when she was sick."

"I've always associated grilled cheese and tomato soup with chicken pox, and now you've reminded me why that is."

The two men chuckled. "Thanks for taking care of Gillian today."

James gave Hunt a warm pat on the shoulder and steered him toward the door, as if he were a teenage date being dismissed for the evening. It was an odd-man-out sensation that shot sadness through Hunt's heart. He wanted to stick around and be a part of their family. He could come clean about his feelings and ask to stay. But that would open a can of worms with James that Gillian might not appreciate.

Nope, best to go on over to Cullen's house and help decorate the miserable little Charlie Brown tree that Cullen had cut down for himself. In a few hours Hunt would call Gillian to check up on her, maybe even head over if she was up to company.

"Drive careful," James urged. "The temperatures are dropping, and there could be icy patches on the roads."

"Fortunately I don't have far to go," Hunt replied as he stepped into the freezing night air. "Call if you need anything at all. I'm only five minutes away."

But even the short drive to Cullen's house seemed like a long road as it took him in the opposite direction from the woman he loved.

CHAPTER NINETEEN

"WHAT DAY IS IT?" Gillian rubbed her temples, feeling like Wile E. Coyote after The Road Runner had dropped an anvil on his head.

"Wednesday," her mother broke the news.

"Are you serious? I've been in this bed three days?"

"For the better part of them, you sure have."

"Why did you let me keep taking those pills?"

"Honey, after the way you cried Sunday morning when the medication had worn off, and you couldn't even hobble to the bathroom, the orthopedist recommended we double your medication until the swelling subsided. Last night your knee seemed much better, so I took the dosage down again. Would you like to sit up and have some coffee and toast?"

"What I'd like is to get into the shower and lose this three-day-old bed head."

Her mother didn't attempt to hide a smile. "I'm sorry to laugh at your expense, but your hair has looked better."

"Please tell me Hunt didn't catch me this way."

"No, of course not. He hasn't been here since Saturday night."

Gillian's heart crumbled like dried flowers. If he hadn't bothered to check on her, how important could she really be in his life? Or maybe he was finally taking her words of rejection seriously.

"Has he even called?"

"You've spoken with him a half-dozen times." Her mother smiled. "I'm not surprised you don't remember. But he completely understood your stupor since he knows how hard you whacked that knee. I told him I'd inform him when you were in shape to receive visitors."

Gillian's mother helped her to the shower

where she sat in a plastic chair underneath the warm spray of water.

"Sitting in a steam bath with a cold gel pack strapped to my knee makes me feel like an oxymoron in the flesh. Thanks for not letting Hunt visit me in this condition."

"All the thanks should go to your father. His quick thinking is the real reason we kept Hunt away from Moore House for a few days."

"What do you mean by that?"

"Karl Gates called Monday morning saying he'd received the permit to start work on the courtyard, and your dad instructed him to take care of the demolition that same day."

"So the well is gone?" She held her breath, suddenly fearing the response.

Her mother nodded. "It's been filled in and covered over as if it was never there. The odor is gone, too, so that space isn't offensive anymore. Once a tile floor is laid, there won't be a trace of the well left."

Even in the steamy shower Gillian felt a chill. The deed was done. Evil spirits hadn't split the earth open or brought the roof down on their heads. Gillian shut off the water and eased to a standing position. Her mother wrapped her in a fluffy robe, helped her to a vanity bench and began to towel-dry her hair.

"What about the stones?"

"Karl's men were able to chip away the mortar and save the rocks that were aboveground. They're in the barn. Dad figured you might want to recycle them someplace else on the property."

"That's a smart idea. I appreciate that Dad gave the go-ahead for me, and I'm glad I slept through it so I wouldn't have regrets."

Meredith took the towel away from Gillian's face so she could look into her eyes. "Did he make the right decision? You and I talked about it on several occasions, and you seemed certain. Karl said he got the same orders from you, or James would never have agreed."

Gillian hated the worry in her mother's voice. She caught both of her hands and squeezed them tightly.

"Mom, I absolutely believe it was the

right thing to do. But Karl insisted Hunt would be upset when he found out."

"He's already discovered it. It was probably best your dad handled that, too."

Gillian dropped her face into her hands. How much worse could this situation get?

"Tell me everything," she mumbled.

"The two workmen who did the job on Monday filled in their wives about it, and by Tuesday morning it was Facebook fodder."

"So *everybody* in town has heard about it already?"

"Basically, but let's think this through. The property has been empty for decades, so it's not as if there were guided tours pointing out the Caddo well. It was mostly legend, and once people get the word out that it's gone, that'll be the end of it."

"Have you spoken with Hunt?"

"No, but your father has. He tried to mitigate the problem by taking responsibility for razing the well."

"Dad shouldn't have done that, but I appreciate his intentions. This was my decision, and I'll own the outcome with Hunt.

Has there been any sort of local media coverage?"

Her mother patted Gillian's back, the only comfort a parent can offer in some situations.

"Not so far. It wasn't exactly a newsworthy event. The city granted the permit, so it's a nonissue for the media. Even so, you have a Caddo sit-in at the gate, and they might be there for a while."

Gillian closed her eyes and let her chin drop to her chest. "Oh, Mom, what sort of chain reaction have I set in motion? When Rachel hears about this she might cancel the booking."

"There's no reason to panic." Meredith's voice was soft and reassuring as she sat beside her daughter on the bench. "Rachel and Buzz have been the subject of gossip and paparazzi all their lives. A few protesters won't make them change their wedding plans, not when they've waited all these years to make it official."

"You're probably right, but I have to do some damage control with them. *And* with Hunt, if he'll listen to me."

"Why don't you give Rachel a call and explain what's happened? Remind her that you couldn't take her out into the courtyard, because it smelled like a skunk crawled in a hole and died, which is probably true. She's a businesswoman. She'll understand."

"Rachel! I was supposed to talk to her about the menu two days ago!"

"Hunt spoke to her and took care of everything."

He'd offered to take care of a lot of stuff for her before she'd destroyed that infernal well. Now she'd be lucky if he hadn't sabotaged everything instead.

"Since I'm lucid again, I've got to get into the game myself."

What should she do? The choices were limited. She could get in the bed and put her head under the covers, she could ignore the local fallout and hope for the best, or she could deal with the situation head-on like the hotelier she claimed she wanted to be.

How would her father react in her situation? It was easy enough to ask him, but she knew instinctively by now. He'd make a call immediately, explain away the issue and offer the guest some unexpected perk to thank them for their continued loyalty.

"I know what I need to do, Mom."

"How can I help?"

"You can get me over to the chaise, find my cell phone and then make me a grilled cheese sandwich."

"With tomato soup?"

"No, thanks. I'm not sick," Gillian insisted.

Unless worried sick counted.

"Why don't you just tell Gillian you love her?" Cullen badgered Hunt.

"It's not that simple. Saying the words out loud won't make our differences go away, and it'll complicate things even more."

"You don't know that for sure. Putting your feelings on the table—no pun intended—may be just what you should do to start moving forward again. Right now you're hung in limbo, waiting for life to happen to you instead of taking the initiative like you've always done."

"You're one to talk," Hunt scoffed. "You've been a college student for fifteen years. When are you gonna get on with *your* life?"

"Here's the difference, little bro. I'm happy. You're not."

Hunt shoved his palms in the hip pockets of his Wranglers and paced the length of Cullen's study. The fact that the room was filled with volumes of wisdom only served to make him feel more stupid for losing control of his future.

"You're right. I'm not happy, and it all started when Gillian showed up and bought Pap's place."

"That doesn't make Gilly the bad guy or the source of your misery. She's been more agreeable to our wishes than we ever expected she would at the beginning. Look how often she's listened to reason from you."

"Tell that to the Caddos camped at the entrance to Temple Territory. They're outraged over what's happened."

"Oh, Hunt. That's just a bunch of old

country boys who call themselves The Tribe. They tailgate every Sunday during football season and take their families camping on South Padre for spring break. Those fellas will use any excuse to sit around a campfire together, including a protest."

"What about the Caddo well? It was important enough for Pap to build his estate around, and now it's full of concrete."

"Take a seat, will ya, Hunt? You're wearing out the rug that Alma put down there to cover the spot where *I* wore out the carpet underneath it."

Hunt flopped into the leather chair beside the massive desk strewn with his brother's research stuff. Hunt's righteous indignation was waning beneath the sense of Cullen's arguments.

"You might have noticed that I care a lot about history," Cullen began to explain.

Hunt snorted laughter at the understatement.

"Okay, I'm on the obsessive side when it comes to studying the past. But that should tell you something. If I'm not bothered by the destruction of that smelly pile of rocks, then you probably shouldn't be, either. There was never any evidence that would support making it a landmark, or the East Texas Historical Society would have slapped a placard on it a hundred years ago."

"Then why was it so important to Pap?"

"That's another mystery about the old man that we may never understand. When a culture wants something significant to be remembered, they find a way to leave a legacy. I can't say what caused Pap to preserve that old well, but if it wasn't important enough to leave the story behind, then it sure isn't important enough to steal your happiness."

"But there was something special, something sacred about the ground around the well."

"Only because you made it so by taking comfort there, Hunt. I did the same thing with Daddy's study. When you took your bedroll to sleep beside the well, I took mine to sleep beside his bookshelf. We were kids, and we found peace the only way we knew how. But we're grown men now, and neither one of us has to cling to a patch of earth anymore to remind us of Daddy and Mama."

"You make a solid case," Hunt muttered.

"What was that again?" Cullen goaded him to speak up.

"You're right, okay!" Hunt gave in to his brother's logic.

"Of course I'm right. Now go take care of that other business before you get side-tracked again. How long do you figure it'll take?"

"Only a couple of days, but with it being the holidays, I may have to attend a few family gatherings to get the job done. I'll be asking for a lot, and I can't just make a call or show up for fifteen minutes and expect people to accommodate me."

"You go do whatever you have to do. We'll still be here when you get home. Since you won't be around to cook dinner on Christmas Day, you can make it up to us with *two* turkeys next year." Cullen rubbed his palms in anticipation. "One roasted and one deep-fried."

GILLIAN WAS HOLDING her cell, rehearsing what she planned to say when Rachel returned her call. The phone buzzed, Hunt's number popped up on the caller ID and then his voice came through the speaker.

"I took a chance you might truly be awake this time."

If it hadn't been for the knee brace keeping her leg locked in place, she might have jumped to her feet with a case of nerves. Gillian's heart lurched at the baritone she'd grown to love, but she didn't hear the anger she expected.

"You're right. I am finally out of the drug-induced fog. And I apologize for the way I must have sounded during the past few calls. I can't remember a thing."

"I assure you that, even under the influence, you were always a lady."

"Now you're on to the fact that I'm a cheap date. I can't drink more than two glasses of wine, and pain medication renders me useless. I should have cut the prescription in half from the very first dose."

"Don't let it worry you. You obviously needed it for the pain. How's the knee?"

"The swelling is going down, but after trying to take a few steps this morning, I understand the reason for the brace and crutches. I can't take any weight on this leg at all."

"That shouldn't come as a shock. You may be a skinny little thing, but your knee took the full force of your body weight on a surface made of stone. In that situation, the stone is usually the winner, because it's hard, meant to last forever and stay right where it is. Unless, of course, somebody decides to bring in a bulldozer, and then the stone won't have much chance."

"Okay, Hunt, enough with the wordplay. Go ahead and say what you have to say, and get it over with."

A sharp rap on her suite door that could only belong to her father interrupted Gillian's intention to get this confrontation over with.

"You seem to have company," Hunt commented.

"Just hold on a minute, please." She muted the cell phone and called out, "Dad, it's okay to come in. I'm decent."

The antique door hinges squeaked. A

face with eyes the color of slate appeared from behind the solid core door.

She yanked her quilt even higher over modest flannel pajamas. "Why didn't you say you were out there?"

"I figured it would be best to share the news after the fact. You know how that is, don't you, Gilly?"

CHAPTER TWENTY

"I MOST CERTAINLY DO," she answered his impertinent question. "Sometimes in life, no matter how you plan for the best and prepare for the worst, you find yourself in a situation you hadn't anticipated."

Gillian watched as Hunt closed the door behind him and took a seat on the sofa near the fireplace. He was only a few feet from where she reclined on the chaise, trying not to appear as frumpy as she felt in a plaid pajama top and her useless leg propped up on throw pillows. His cologne was enticing, even from a distance, and he was perfectly turned out, as always.

The steamy mirrors in the bathroom hadn't lied. She looked frightful. Her mother had dragged a fresh shirt over her head and run a brush through her wet hair, but that was all the grooming they'd been able to do. At least she was clean and she'd given her teeth a good scrubbing in the shower.

"You're exactly where I left you three days ago," he observed.

Gillian pointed toward the bed. "I'm pretty sure that's where I've been most of the past seventy-two hours. I remember you bringing me home and my parents coming in, but everything until this morning is a blur."

"Has your father brought you up to speed on the work that's been done while you were getting your beauty rest?"

"Hunt, as I already suggested, go ahead and have your say. Get it off your chest so we can move on, one way or the other." She tried to sound as resolute and matter-of-fact as possible, determined to disguise the fact that his *moving on* was her greatest fear.

He sat forward on the cushion, his boots pressed into the carpet, elbows resting on solid thighs while his hands dangled between his knees. With his eyes focused on some point between his toes, it was difficult to discern any expression on his face. He held that pensive pose for several long seconds. When Hunt's gaze finally sought hers, there was an unmistakable gleam of tears in his eyes.

Gillian had expected any number of reactions, but this one was not on the list. Under different circumstances she'd have moved to sit beside him, put her arm around his shoulders and hold him close until he got through the emotional moment. But she'd been the one to cause the sadness, and she wasn't exactly mobile. So she stayed put and crafted her words carefully.

"Hunt, I'm sorry this has affected you so strongly, but it's not personal. It was a business decision and nothing more. That eyesore was smack in the middle of a spot where I need to build, and it had to be eliminated. The city gave me permission, and I gave the go-ahead."

"So this wasn't something your father ordered without your knowledge?"

"Absolutely not. I may have been in a drug-induced stupor when the work was accomplished, but it was done at my direction. Dad was trying to spare me some heat, but he shouldn't have misled you when he said he'd been the one to give Karl the go-ahead. I did that almost a week ago."

"Karl knew about this?" Hunt seemed incredulous. He probably felt betrayed by his friend.

"Yes, and he did his best to talk me out of it. But the destruction of the well has been in the architectural plans all along. The roofline is going to be extended over the courtyard, and a wall of glass block will be built to enclose the space to create the spa."

"That's what was in the drawings that you wouldn't show me," he deduced.

She nodded. "We got to this point in the renovations much sooner than I expected. The well was a health hazard and out of place in an upscale boutique hotel. It had to go. Surely you can understand ranking a business decision over a personal preference."

"Of course I can," he admitted.

"Then why does this seem to cut you so deeply?"

He glanced away for a moment. She

watched his chest expand with a deep breath.

"You don't trust me." He shook his head. "Not completely."

"I don't trust anybody other than my parents completely."

"I'm well aware of that now."

"Hunt, what did you expect? It's not like we've known one another all our lives. It's only been a short time. Even so, consider how much things have changed between us. We've gone from zero to ninety in sixty seconds. From open animosity to partnership, from strangers to…"

"To what?"

"I'm not even sure what name to put on this *relationship* that's developed between us. But I am sure it's weighted in your favor, and that makes it unfair to me."

She had his attention. The muscles in his jaws worked as he gritted his teeth. As long as he was moving through the hurt feelings, she might as well say the rest.

"Hunt, how can you ask for such a level of trust when you can't even say you'll still be part of my life in six weeks? When you can't guarantee we'll occupy the same five hundred square miles next year? When, predictably, you put more stock in maintaining the stuff in this place than in caring about the woman who owns it?"

"Are you finished?"

"Not just yet."

He inclined his head and swept one open palm, a sign to continue.

"I admit I was closed off to your suggestions in the beginning, but as my mind opened up, so did my heart. I saw the wisdom in keeping your pap's spirit alive here, in letting some of his legacy find a home with me. And in response you went shopping for another opportunity, hell-bent on finding the next challenge for the Cowboy Chef. And then you gripe because I don't trust you completely."

"Is that all?" he asked.

"Why? Are you in a hurry to leave? Do you have some place more important to jet off to? Maybe a job interview to be Chef de Cuisine in London or Rio? Anyplace would be better than here with me, I suppose."

Her voice was unsteady. She heard it

quiver as she did what she'd told Hunt to do, revealing true feelings. But while she'd gotten a few things off her chest, it didn't even scratch the surface of all that was in her heart.

WOMEN WERE NEXT to impossible to read, but Hunt was pretty sure Gillian was saying she loved him without *saying* she loved him. She'd called him predictable, thought she could anticipate his next move, which meant she expected him to lob a grenade right back at her. So he did the unexpected.

He closed the space between them with two steps and dropped to one knee before Gillian. He'd have gathered her into his arms, but a pair of metal crutches leaning against the side of that chaise thing blocked his path. So he settled for gathering her hands between his. Her long, graceful fingers were cold, so he bent his head, exhaled a warm breath and kissed them sweetly.

"Gillian, I need to ask you a question." His voice was soft.

Violet eyes flew wide with alarm.

"This is hardly the time or place! I'm

not ready!" She made an effort to tug her hands free but his grip increased. "What on earth are you doing, Hunt?"

"Not what you think, that's for sure." He laughed out loud. "Not today, anyway."

Gillian struggled again, but he wasn't letting her go. Not now, not ever. He was gonna hang on to this woman for dear life. But she was right; he had to take it more slowly.

"Will you stop trying to get away, Hop-Along Cassidy?" He poked fun at her disabled knee.

"So are you on one knee just to harass me on my own level?" Gillian brought him back to the reason for his posture.

"That's partially what I had in mind." He let the silly smile slip from his lips. "But mostly I want to get your full attention, so you'll take me seriously."

"What is it, Hunt?" The intensity of her stare pierced to his very soul. "What's wrong?"

"Oh, Gilly. Everything's wrong, and everything's right all in the same breath." As he cupped her fingers gently they began to warm, just as he was warming to his subject.

"First, I'm at a place in my career where I can be the star of the show, demanding the big bucks. But instead, I'm drawn to a small venue. It has a lot of future-earning potential, but right now it can't really afford me. And second, something I always believed I wanted has slipped through my fingers. I should ache with the loss, but instead I feel pride, because in the hands of someone more capable than me, it's becoming greater than I ever imagined it could be."

Gratitude welled in Gillian's eyes, and he said a silent thank-you to his twin who'd realized before Hunt had that the moment had come to speak his heart. He leaned close and inhaled the enticing scent of grilled cheese, and then pressed a tender kiss to the mouth that tasted of butter and salt. As he released her hands, pulled away and sat on his heels, she caught his face between her palms.

She urged him closer again and whispered, "What's the third thing?"

"The third thing is really the first thing." He paused, searched her face. Then he pressed his forehead to Gillian's and closed his eyes, unable to continue.

"Go on," she encouraged.

"I'm falling in love for the first time in my life, and the woman of my dreams is so busy fulfilling her own dreams that she doesn't have much of herself left for me."

"Oh, Hunt," Gillian whispered, the sadness in her tone telling him what he'd been afraid of hearing.

He rushed on. "So it shouldn't come as a surprise that I kept my options open and my eye on the future. If you won't fault me for that, I won't fault you for reserving trust to a very few."

"Gillian?" Meredith was at the door. "The call you've been waiting for has come through on the business line. Can you talk or would you prefer I say you're not available?"

"I'm sorry, but I have to take this," she said to Hunt.

"So there you have it." He shrugged and then stood. "I'll just be going, so you can get on with more important things."

Gillian grabbed his hand, preventing him from moving away.

"Mother, give me sixty seconds and then put the call through, please." Her mother nodded. To Hunt, Gillian said, "I need you to stay and listen, okay? I've been rehearsing what to tell Rachel for the past hour, and I could use your moral support and coaching. Would you mind?"

"Of course not."

Ringing pierced the quiet and buttons flashed on a nearby multiline phone beyond Gillian's reach.

"If you'll press the speaker line for me, I'll take it from there."

"Gillian?" Rachel's familiar accent came from the phone.

"Well, hello there!" A smile in Gillian's tone disguised the trepidation Hunt found in her eyes.

"Is everything going to be okay when we get there?" Rachel's voice echoed with concern.

"Could you be more specific?"

"Hunt mentioned a couple of days ago that you'd taken a spill and buggered up your knee."

"Oh, that."

"What do you mean by 'oh, that'? Is there more?"

"A bit more, yes, but nothing we can't manage."

"Please don't say the news has leaked and the bloody paparazzi are already camped out down there."

"No, Rachel, it's not the press. But, now that you mention it, we do have a few guys sort of camped out."

Hunt stood close by and silently nodded encouragement. Gillian explained the situation as if her script had been written by a spin doctor. She kept to the facts, minimized the brouhaha and assured Rachel repeatedly that the minor incident would not impact their plans.

"I hadn't intended to bring this up, and please don't take it as a threat, Gillian, but I have a backup reservation out in Vegas if the worst happens."

Hunt's gut twisted, but he was certain it was nothing compared to what Gillian must be experiencing.

"Please, Rachel, don't go with another venue. We're prepared to give you what you've always dreamed of and some surprises you hadn't even imagined for yourselves."

"Surprises?" Rachel perked up. "Tell me more."

While Gillian spoke of holiday decorations and gourmet touches, Hunt grabbed her notepad, scribbled quickly and held it up where she could see. Gillian shook her head and mouthed *no,* but Hunt pointed again to the note, adamant that she go along with what he'd written. She closed her eyes in a sign of surrender and then spoke again.

"And the biggest surprise of all, Rachel, is an unexpected guest or two who will give that perfect touch of envy to everyone who's not on your guest list. I guarantee the next day you'll be the talk of the Lone Star State, if not the darling of the national press."

"How exciting and clever of you, Gillian. I hope it's some really fabulous Texan like Willie Nelson or J. R. Ewing."

Hunt rolled his eyes and smiled, not at all sure the Aussie beauty was aware the Ewings were fictional characters.

"You have my word, you won't be disappointed. Trust me to do the job you're paying for, as well as a little mystery for your wedding day."

Gillian and Hunt gave one another a thumbs-up.

"Alrighty then, my dear. You've convinced me that everything is in capable hands. Do take care and follow doctor's orders. You won't want to be limping around during the reception when I'm introducing you to royalty from London, Hollywood and New York."

"Rachel, should we hire additional security? Will there truly be royalty among your guests?"

"Only in their own minds." Rachel laughed. "And I'm quite certain they will find your amazing little hotel as charming as Buzz and I have."

"I CAN'T LET you do this, Hunt."

The call ended, and he'd returned to sit on the sofa.

"It's a bit late for that, Gilly. And besides, it was brewing in my mind before this ever happened. I wouldn't have suggested it if I didn't believe I could pull it off."

"But it's Christmas! You can't just call celebrity friends and expect them to drop everything and come to East Texas."

"That's why I'm going to do it in person." He checked his watch. "I can't stay any longer."

"But you hate to fly, especially on a holiday."

"A cowboy's gotta do what a cowboy's gotta do," he teased.

"You already had this planned, didn't you? Before we even talked, before Rachel's call, you'd made up your mind to do this."

He nodded.

"But why? You were angry with me over the well, and hurt that I hadn't trusted you about my plans. Why would you do this for me?"

"Because that's what you do for the person you love."

He hesitated for a moment, giving her

time to return the confession. But she only stared wide-eyed at him, so he continued.

"My daddy worked long hours, but he always managed to bring home flowers for Mama. And even when she was upset with him for putting his duty to the hospital before his family, she always made sure his needs were met, and she taught us to tell him how much we appreciated him. I lost my folks far too soon, but their quiet witness of love for one another was a seed they sowed in us very early."

"That's the way it should be between married people because they're committed to the relationship, Hunt. They're obligated to support each other. But it's not your responsibility to get me out of a tight spot, and I don't want you to feel bound in any way to take advantage of your personal contacts to help me out."

"Did you understand what I just said? Did you hear the part about duty and turn a deaf ear to the part about love?"

He sounded frustrated, and she feared she'd screwed up any chance they had for a future together.

Gillian held out her hand, her eyes pleading with words she wasn't sure how to say. He didn't hesitate. Hunt got on one knee beside her again, but this time there was no humor in his voice when he spoke.

"What do you want, Gillian? If it's not me, I can deal with that, but I need to know if I'm even on your short list."

CHAPTER TWENTY-ONE

"MY SHORT LIST?" A spurt of laughter erupted. "As if there's a gaggle of suitors lined up for my attention."

"There might as well be with Moore House as my competition."

"Hunt, why does a relationship have to become a competition?"

"It doesn't! That's what I'm trying to tell you, darlin'. You don't have to choose, but you do have to ease back on the intensity of your focus. It just so happens that in this case you can have your cake and eat it, too, but you've got to find the time to take a bite."

"And I intend to do just that as soon as I—"

"As soon as you what?" he snapped. "Complete every detail of the hotel? Work so many hours that it threatens your health? Get the rug yanked out from under you so you're forced to stop and smell the honey-suckle?"

She could hear his exasperation growing.

"Talk to your parents, for crying out loud. I bet they'll say they wish they'd been forced out years ago, because now they're doing the things in life that are important to them."

"But I *am* doing what's important," she insisted.

"Okay, do whatever you want. You will anyway." Hunt stood but hesitated to move toward the door.

"Are you on your way to the airport right now?"

"No, I'm headed out to Mac's house for dinner. I have a nine o'clock flight tomorrow morning for New York to visit one of my friends who's made it big on TV. He's invited me to have Christmas Eve dinner with his family. Then I'll spend Christmas Day flying cross-country to spend some time with a chef I met on the show, who's got several restaurants in L.A."

"Do you really believe they'll do this for you?"

He smiled.

"I've known them to do crazier things for an expensive bottle of wine. They're both great chefs, but mostly they're cool guys who love a challenge, and this is just the sort of opportunity that gives their lives the unpredictability they love."

"You'll have to tell them about Rachel and Buzz, won't you?"

"Yes, but they can be trusted. And they can come to town with a full staff and camera crew. They're accustomed to being stealth, so nobody will even notice until the challenge is thrown down. I'm excited to see them again. It's been a while."

"But you'll miss the holiday, Hunt. What about your brothers?"

"It won't be the first Christmas we've spent apart. Alma's agreed to take over in the kitchen and one less fork in the battle for the turkey's tail means a lower risk of injury."

Gillian closed her eyes and leaned her head against the chaise. The throbbing in her knee intensified, made worse by the fact that the injury was her own stupid fault. And instead of a holiday with his family, Hunt was going to spend the days before and after Christmas doing the one thing he dreaded: flying from Texas to New York to California and back again. If she'd left that blasted Caddo well alone for a few days longer, she'd be having the unforgettable Christmas Eve she'd envisioned. With the man she loved. But she'd gone full speed ahead, doing whatever she wanted, just as Hunt had accused her of doing. So lousing up Christmas was all her fault, too.

She should seize this very moment to tell Hunt what was in her heart. But then what? He'd race away, determined to save the day for her, even though she didn't deserve his help, much less his love.

No, sending him off with a halfhearted declaration of love was unfair to both of them. What she had to say concerned their forever. It had waited this long, and it would wait a few more days.

"Hunt, before you leave, would you mind helping me to my feet? This brace strapped to my knee is about as accommodating as a two-by-four."

"Sure. All you had to do was ask."

When had this man become so agreeable? What had happened to the know-it-all cook she'd hired to give her guests that touch of arrogance and sophistication they craved? How was it that the Cowboy Chef had climbed down off his high horse to cater to the woman who'd come between him and the legacy of his grandfather?

As she posed these silent conundrums to herself, Hunt gently helped her to a standing position, placed a crutch beneath each arm and stepped back to give her room to navigate. She wobbled, dropped a crutch and risked pitching forward into his arms. He caught her easily, as she'd been certain he would, and then she shamelessly tipped her face to his.

"Kiss me, Hunt." She was desperate. "Pretty please?"

"In that case…" His words trailed away as his mouth covered hers.

His kiss was an extension of the puzzle she'd been mulling over in her mind. One moment Hunt's lips were light and tender against hers, the next demanding and possessive. Gillian pulled her body as close as she dared and reveled in the joy of Hunt's embrace. She returned his kiss, matching the hungry emotion that grew as the moments passed with the two of them at the center of the universe. She was at home in his arms, and she never wanted the feeling to end.

HUNT BROKE THE SPELL. He raised his head from the lips he hoped to kiss for the rest of his life. Instead of indulging again, he settled feather-soft kisses along her stubborn jaw, across the bridge of her perfect nose and beside the lids of Gillian's stunning violet eyes.

He leaned his head back and took in the vision of his beloved. Her cheeks were flushed pink from their intimacy, but the nearly translucent skin beneath her eyes was dark with fatigue. Even after several days of rest she was still physically and mentally worn out. And he'd added to her worry by showing up and demanding answers he already knew.

She was a woman with a plan and she would not be deterred. Well, now he had a plan of his own and it was time to make tracks.

He traced the apple of her cheek lightly with a knuckle. She opened her eyes, an intensity in their depths he'd never before noticed there.

"I'm leaving town just in time."

"How can you say that when tomorrow is Christmas Eve?"

"If I stayed, you wouldn't get the rest you should have, and right now that's critical to your knee mending, especially if you expect to wear some fancy high heels with your crutches for the wedding."

"Hmm, that's a good way to show off my Louboutin pumps. One red sole turned upward, begging to be admired. There's merit in that idea."

"Just promise me you'll stick with the pain meds, let your mama take care of you and let your daddy take care of Moore House."

When she didn't nod in agreement, he gave her body a little shake. "Promise me, Gillian," Hunt demanded.

"I promise. I suppose the least I can do is agree with you when you're leaving town on my account just at the moment when everyone else is heading home for the holidays."

"Let me ask you a question, and tell me the truth."

She nodded but her forehead scrunched in doubt.

"Was that a pity kiss?"

Her head fell back, and she went nearly limp in his arms with laughter. He supported the weight of her body while she enjoyed his question.

"Well?" He waited with a smile on his face while she halfheartedly composed herself.

"If that was a pity kiss, then I'm the governor of Texas."

"I've met our governor and the mental image of kissing him on the lips is quite revolting. So I'm going to interpret your response to mean you didn't kiss me just to be nice."

"I kiss my uncle Buck to be nice. I kissed you because I had to take advantage of the few moments we have before you leave. I hope that's okay."

"Darlin', it would be okay if you took advantage of me like that every day for the rest of our lives."

"Shh." Gillian pressed her fingertips to his lips. "Let's talk about that when you're not checking your watch as if you have a bus to catch."

He pressed her palm to his lips and then folded it close to his heart. "I'd take you with me this evening if you were up to it."

"But I'm not, so you can't. Go on and be with your family tonight, and I'll see you in a few days."

He reached for the crutches that had fallen to the floor and handed them to her.

"Thank you, Hunt." She secured her balance on her support foot. "Merry Christmas."

"Merry Christmas, my darlin'." His voice clogged with pent up emotion.

Then he turned and slipped through the door, not daring to look back.

"SURPRISE!" CULLEN SINGSONGED AS Hunt walked through Mac's front door.

"He knew we'd be here, ya big dope." The sofa creaked as Joiner leaned to frog Cullen's arm with the deadly knuckle punch the brothers had perfected in their youth. "With your lack of common sense, you woulda made a good Aggie."

Cullen rubbed his bicep. "Are you referring to that university down in College Station that regularly beat your team like a borrowed mule when you played for Texas?"

Joiner shook his head in disgust. "You can't give it a rest for a single day, can you?"

"What was that game called again? The one where you chase a ball up and down the field? Was it football? No, you wouldn't pick the game the whole state of Texas plays." Cullen tapped his chin and pretended to be thinking. "Was it baseball? No, you wouldn't pick a game your little brothers excelled in 'cause we'd kick your tail. What was that game called again?"

"Marco!" McCarthy called from the kitchen.

"Polo! That's it! Polo! The game that left you a penniless sucker."

"When are you boys going to grow up?" Alma shouted above the laughter. "The last time I checked, you were all thirtysomethings."

Cullen and Mac hooted for the umpteenth time over the Marco Polo pun they'd been using on poor Joiner since the day he'd first picked up a mallet.

But Hunt understood his older brother's passion.

He felt the same when he tied on an apron and took hold of a knife. It may not look natural on the outside but it was a perfect fit on the inside. The big difference was he'd made cooking work as a career. Joiner had gambled on a life in the high-stakes world of polo and lost just about everything.

Hunt made the rounds of the big lake house, hugging necks and exchanging slaps on the back. This was family. This was home. This was Christmas. And no matter how exotic the location or how high the salary he could find elsewhere in the world, he was always drawn here to these people in this small town.

"Alma, you didn't have to cook tonight *and* Christmas Day."

"La cocina para mis marcas familiares mí feliz," she said, reminding him she was happiest when she was cooking for her family.

"And we're all grateful to be on the receiving end of your good cheer."

He showed his appreciation by taking the carving knife from Mac and doing what he could to hide the damage his oldest brother had done turning a perfectly roasted bird into a sacrificial turkey.

"I would never pass up the chance to feed my boys. Someday, *si el Señor bueno lo hace tan,* you will have wives of your own, and you won't need old Alma."

"That could happen much sooner than you think, Alma." Cullen draped an arm around his twin.

Hunt cut his eyes toward Cullen, a clear message to keep his mouth shut.

"It's no use, little bro," Mac drawled. "We were all watching you two at my party, and even though it took a few PhDs for Cullen to catch on, we could see for ourselves how smitten you are with the lovely Miss Moore."

"*Smitten* won't cover it. He looked at her as if he wanted to sop her up with a biscuit," Joiner teased.

"Will you guys give it a rest, please? I didn't drive out here for a dose of abuse, especially since I'm about to get a healthy ration from my friends on each coast."

"Help Felix get the meal on the table, and while we eat, you can tell us all about your plans." Alma gave orders, all five men did as they were told and nobody got hurt.

CHAPTER TWENTY-TWO

"MERRY CHRISTMAS, BEAUTIFUL."

"Good morning!" Gillian's pulse raced at the sound of Hunt's voice on the phone. "Where are you?"

"I'm at JKF, sitting in a coffee shop out on the concourse, waiting for my 767 to show up."

She glanced toward the mantel clock. Just before 9:00 a.m.

"When does your flight leave?"

"Half an hour ago."

"Oh, I'm sorry." She grimaced at the idea of Hunt being stuck in an impersonal airport on the most important family holiday of all. "What a lousy way to spend Christmas morning."

"It's not so bad. Everybody's in a pleasant mood, which is pretty unusual for an airport. There's music and decorations, and people giving out samples of fruitcake and potato latkes. Not exactly gourmet fare, but they're free and come with a smile, so I've accepted them and said, 'Thank you very kindly,' just like my mama taught me."

"You have a great attitude for a guy who's missing out on the festivities at home."

"Well, I spent last evening in Manhattan with my friend Robby and his family. He was so gracious to invite me to join them for dinner. I should have realized it was a setup."

"Who did the cooking?" She smiled, suspecting what he was about to say.

"Who do you think?" His warm laughter echoed across the miles and chased the chill from her room. "Robby had a feeling I was coming all this way to ask a favor, and he let me walk right into a trap. He had twenty people to feed, and his caterer had come down with the flu. I was happy to step in, but he sure enjoyed being the one to deliver the news that I had to sing for my supper."

"Did he agree to come down to Kilgore

next week?" She held her breath, certain the celebrity chef already had plans.

"Of course. He said he'd make the trip even before I told him who your guests would be. Once he found out it was Rachel and Buzz, he said he'd be there with sleigh bells on. There's just one catch."

"What's that?" She hid her eyes behind her hand, afraid of what was coming.

"He wants to bring a small crew to film some footage for the next season of his show."

She shook her head. "Rachel will never go along with that."

"If she won't agree, then she won't be on camera with Robby. And as much as they claim to love their privacy, Rachel and Buzz are publicity hogs."

"Excellent point," Gillian agreed.

"Anything taped now won't air for months. Their marriage will be old news by then, and they'll be lucky to squeeze some more press coverage out of it. Especially on a food channel with an entirely different fan base."

"It makes sense, they might go for it."

"What about you?"

"I think it's wonderful!"

"But will you agree to let Robby film at Moore House?"

She took a moment to consider what the photographs and videos of the property would look like in the winter. The miles of outdoor lights her father and Felix had strung through the trees would cast a surreal mask, drawing the eye away from brown grass and barren limbs. The interior would be stunning with ivory, silver and ocean-blue, the colors Rachel had chosen for her wedding theme. And the thousands of blooming flowers Gillian had purchased to carry out her vision would be a living rainbow before the camera lens. The hard work of so many to restore the home was fresh and unscarred and it would be on display for the world to see.

"I would be honored to have his film crew here with us. I only wish there was an empty suite to offer."

"He's got a tricked-out bus that he and his crew use to tour the country, so don't worry about rooms."

Gillian heard a rush of noisy activity at the other end of the line.

"Hunt, are you still there?"

"Yes, but the desk just called a gate change. Everybody around me jumped up, grabbed their kids and carry-on bags and took off down the concourse as if the checkered flag had been waved at a stock-car race."

"I guess you have to go, too, huh?" Her spirits plunged. He'd be on a plane for hours, traveling across three time zones and thousands of miles farther away from her.

The moment the door had closed behind him the day before, she'd begun to experience a deep ache, and it had nothing to do with her banged-up knee.

Her heart was hurting. Missing Hunt. "Yeah, I guess I'd better get going. It won't be much warmer when I land in San Francisco, but at least it won't be blowing snow."

"Will you bring me a bottle of Sonoma County merlot and some Ghirardelli chocolate?"

"As long as you've got me working the holiday clearance table at the San Francisco airport gift shop, would you also like a loaf of day-old sourdough bread?" he teased.

"Yes, please. Oh, and a 49ers cap if you can find one."

"You're really pressing your luck, darlin'."

"Could I ask for one more thing?"

"Name it."

"Would you call me tonight?"

"I'd already planned on it, figuring you'd be dying to hear about the crying baby or the old man with bad breath who'll probably occupy the seat beside me for the next seven hours."

"Thank you again for doing this for me, Hunt. You're an amazing man with a giving heart."

"Aw, shucks, ma'am." He dragged out the words in his best Texas drawl. "My motives aren't entirely altruistic. There's a win in this for me if I play my cards right."

"How's that?"

"I'll earn the favor of the woman I love."

"You already have my favor."

"I want more than thanks and gratitude, Gillian. I want you to love me right back, and more than anything."

Her mind went into turmoil each time he spoke of love. She not only shared his feelings, she truly trusted him more than anyone in her life. So why was it impossible to put one word in front of the other and tell him that?

"I don't know what to say," she whispered honestly.

"Say you'll keep an open mind. That's worked out well so far." There was more noise in the background. "Listen, I've gotta go. Call you later?"

"Please."

"Merry Christmas, Gilly."

"Merry Christmas, Hunt." She pressed a key to end the call.

"I love you right back, and more than anything," she told the empty room.

HUNT BOARDED THE crowded aircraft, shoved his carry-on bag overhead and climbed into the middle seat in economy class he'd been lucky to get at the last minute.

"Excuse me, sir. Are you Hunt Temple?"

He glanced to the aisle where the flight attendant had paused from her work of closing storage compartments and checking to ensure that seat belts were fastened. She smiled to encourage his response.

"Why, yes, ma'am, guilty as charged."

"Would you collect your belongings and come with me, please?"

Without giving him the opportunity to question her instructions, she moved away. Hunt shrugged at the passengers around him and climbed back into the aisle.

"I'm already in trouble, and we haven't even pushed away from the gate."

To the sound of snickering, he grabbed his bag and headed toward the front of the plane, wondering what he'd done to be singled out like an errant schoolboy.

"Let me take that for you, Chef Temple." The uniformed woman he'd been following reached for his canvas bag. "You'll be much more comfortable up here."

Another flight attendant invited him to take one of the empty first-class seats, then offered him a hot towel and a mimosa.

"Welcome aboard, Chef Temple." She gave him a sunny smile. "I'm Dorothy. Molly and I recognized you when you passed through the cabin, but we wanted to check the manifest to be sure. We try to take care of our VIP guests when we can."

"It's awful nice of you ladies to look out for an old cowboy." He exaggerated his drawl to make them smile. Women outside of the South especially enjoyed hearing his Texas accent.

"Chef, you're neither old nor a cowboy, but we love the effort just the same."

He relaxed into a seat without another passenger at his elbow. "Santa paid me a visit this year after all." He stretched his long legs and sighed with relief.

"We're sorry you're not home with your family today, but Molly and I will do our best to give you a comfortable trip."

The two attendants went about their business and left him to pull his favorite black Stetson down over his eyes, fold his hands across his belt buckle and doze off.

Suddenly, Hunt's head snapped up, sending his hat flying to the floor. A child shrieked somewhere in the cabin, and he reflexively grabbed for the armrests as the 767 bounced hard against a rough sky.

"It's okay," a female beside him reassured, patting his arm to draw his attention from the turbulence. "You've slept through the worst part already. We're almost past it now."

"How long have we been in the air?" He was groggy from deep sleep.

"Over an hour. You were so hard gone that you missed breakfast, but I'm sure they'll bring you a tray if you're hungry."

She retrieved his Stetson from the floor and passed it across the empty seat between them.

"Thank you kindly," he said, and swiped at the brim with his sleeve.

Once the hat was safely back on his head, Hunt sat up straight, caught the attendant's eye and signaled for something to drink. Then he cast a glance toward the Good Samaritan who just happened to be an attractive brunette. Based on her designer clothes, he'd bet she could afford the full price of her first-class ticket. A déjà vu moment pricked at his brain, until he realized that had been the same assumption he'd made about Gillian, and he'd been wrong. He mentally flogged himself for being judgmental.

"Happy holidays, ma'am." He politely offered his hand, and she accepted it, her grip confident.

"Merry Christmas," she responded.

"So we're not being politically correct. Good." He relaxed his spine again. "I get so tired of that nonsense."

"It's enough that we're traveling today. It'd be silly to pretend it's not Christmas," she agreed.

Dorothy brought them each a cup of coffee and placed a basket of fresh muffins and a bowl of berries on Hunt's tray.

"If you'd prefer something more, please get my attention. I kept a plate of eggs Benedict warm for you, just in case."

"Anytime you want a job on terra firma you just holler, and I'll find you a new home, Ms. Dorothy."

"I'll keep that in mind, Chef Temple."

"Chef Hunt Temple? From that cooking show?" the brunette asked.

His eyes widened, amazed at the attention. "That's twice in one day. I should travel more often. Folks back home don't seem to understand that I'm a big celebrity."

"Back home is Texas, right?"

He nodded, his mouth full of banana nut muffin.

"Temple." The brunette seemed to be puzzling something as she squinted, checking him out more closely. "I'm Brenda Shaffer. I'm originally from San Francisco, but I got my master's in marketing from UT a few years ago. I attended an unforgettable lecture on European history by a Dr. Temple. Any relation?"

"Good gravy." Hunt rolled his eyes. "When I tell my brother—after all my efforts to build my own career—that my real claim to fame is being related to Cullen Temple, he's gonna laugh out loud."

"Dr. Cullen Temple. That's him. Texas may be a big state, but it's a small world."

"I'll drink to that," Hunt agreed and raised his coffee cup in salute.

"So what's taking you to San Francisco on Christmas, Chef?"

As much as he wanted to polish off another pastry and fall asleep again, it would be rude. She'd not only recognized him, she'd been a student of Cullen's, so he'd have to behave like a gentleman. Or he'd be in the doghouse with Alma.

Hunt gave her the *Reader's Digest* version of the reason for his trip, carefully avoiding all names.

"You must really love this woman, if you're jetting across the lower forty-eight states to do her a favor."

"I never said my friend was a woman," he insisted.

"It wasn't necessary to spell it out. The tone in your voice and the admiration on your face filled in the blanks for you."

"Okay, I'm busted. She's someone very special to me."

"Is she aware of that? Have you told her?"

"In roundabout ways. I'm not sure she'll

be one hundred percent receptive, so I haven't laid all my cards on the table."

"In other words, you're beating around the bush."

"If I'd wanted to be badgered about my love life, I'd have stayed home with my brothers today," Hunt said with a smile.

"I'm a believer in straight-shooting. Most women are, truthfully. We're just afraid of running men off early in the deal by declaring ourselves too soon. We have to sit quietly and pretend we're not dangling the bait."

"That reminds me of something my daddy said years ago. He told me datin' is like fishin'." Hunt ticked the points off on his fingers. "You've gotta be patient, keep your tackle box full of lures, jiggle the line every now and then to keep things interesting, and never try to set the hook until you know it's all the way in her mouth."

Brenda's brows shot up "*Her* mouth?"

"I meant *it,* in *its* mouth. *The fish's mouth.*" His response was sheepish, apologetic.

"When you get around to telling your

lady friend that you love her, don't repeat the fishing metaphor."

"Not very romantic, is it?"

"Not even a little bit." Her dark eyes lit with a smile. "But funny."

They spent the rest of the flight exchanging amusing stories. Hunt kept his tales impersonal in case someone listening posted what they'd overheard on some social media site.

On the other hand, Brenda was more than willing to offer up details about her home, family and career. By all accounts the lady was somebody important in the Madison Avenue world of advertising, a subject as foreign to Hunt as making mayonnaise from scratch was to Cullen. But Hunt was grateful for such an entertaining distraction. She kept his mind off the bumpy ride as they crossed the Rockies, and had him laughing when he'd normally be gripping the armrests with rigid white knuckles.

They'd just finished French vanilla frozen yogurt and freshly baked oatmeal cookies when Dorothy and Molly began to prepare the cabin for landing.

Hunt spun the hour hand of his watch back in time. "I can't believe we're here already." His only plan for the evening was to take a cab to his hotel where he'd hang out until tomorrow morning when it was time to meet with Gabe.

"Thank you for making it a pleasant trip. I'd have been miserable sitting here alone with only the games on my cell phone for distraction from the turbulence."

The pilot asked everyone to stay seated a few moments longer, until they'd come to a complete stop at the gate.

"I seriously doubt you'd have been either miserable or alone from the way those two flight attendants have kept watch over you."

He craned his neck to see where they'd gone.

"Is that right? I didn't notice."

"That's because they were sitting quietly, pretending not to be dangling the bait."

They were next to deplane.

"May I offer you a ride, Hunt? My car is in the parking garage."

"Thanks, but no. A friend is meeting me," he lied.

Brenda stood and accepted the full-length silver fox fur coat that Dorothy brought from the closet. Hunt watched as Brenda slid her arms inside, pulled the silky pelts close and tossed her chestnut hair over the collar. She reached into the alligator handbag that matched her shoes and withdrew a small white card.

"If your lady friend is not a hundred percent receptive, as I believe she will be once you get up the nerve to speak your mind, you give me a call."

He accepted the card and touched the brim of his hat as she turned away.

Hunt sat down, stared at Brenda Shaffer's contact information and waited until the plane was empty before venturing through the exit and out onto the concourse. He glanced around, saw no familiar faces and tossed the card into a nearby trash can. Gillian Moore already had him hooked more permanently than an eighteen-pound bass on the last day of a fishing tournament.

And Gillian was all the woman—and all the trouble—he could handle.

CHAPTER TWENTY-THREE

"Whoa! Slow down. Slow down."

Hunt tried to calm Gillian over the phone, but she was as close to losing it as he figured she could be.

"Take a deep breath and then start over. I caught the part about the wedding being canceled but give me the details again at a lower decibel level."

Gillian blew her nose and hiccupped before responding.

"Rachel and Buzz got into a fight during their Christmas open house. The party was one of those big deals they throw at their Hampton estate with their kids and neighbors and local celebrities coming and going all day. Anyway, Buzz consumed a little too much mulled cider and let it slip that they'll be married before the week is out. The person he spilled the wassail to happens to write for *Entertainment Magazine*.

When the guy cozied up to Rachel for the details, she threw what you'd call a wall-eyed hissy fit and told the guy hell would freeze over before she'd make it legal with that idiot Buzz."

"Are you sure she wasn't just saying that to throw the writer off the scent?"

"No, Rachel's serious about canceling. She called me herself a couple hours ago with the news. They'll pay the bill, of course, but we've gone to all this planning and work expecting this would be our publicity launch, and it's all going to fall flat."

"Maybe not, Gilly. I'm sure we can turn this situation around. I've got all night to brainstorm before I meet with Gabe in the morning."

"Oh, Hunt!" She was in tears again. "I've been so selfish, I hadn't even stopped to consider all the trouble I've put you through in the past forty-eight hours. I'm so sorry," she blubbered.

"First, my darlin', you didn't put me through any trouble. This was all my idea, and I've done it voluntarily. We'll consider it part of my Christmas gift to you, okay? No harm, no foul.

"And, second, you've got to get past the apologies and the panic, so we can make this work to your advantage. Remember the day the wrong trim was delivered, and we talked about turning lemons into lemon cheesecake? Well, this is the same thing on a grand scale. There's got to be a way to salvage it. Maybe in the light of day Rachel will be more willing to listen to reason."

"Even if she changes her mind, she's lost the element of surprise that was so important to her. She'll never have the ceremony here now that her secret is out."

"Does anybody know about it yet?"

"Just everyone who follows her on Twitter since she tweeted it herself. I guess that was her way of getting *satisfaction,* if you catch my drift."

"Then it'll be picked up by all the news services tomorrow. Did she at least mention Moore House? They say bad publicity is better than no publicity." He was suddenly wishing he'd kept that business card, but not for the reason it was intended. They could use some advice from a marketing professional now.

"I honestly don't know. I wasn't in a position to ask her a lot of questions, and I only learned about the tweet from Dad."

"James? How'd he hear about it?"

"Oh, he follows all kinds of high-profile people. He says he's doing hotel reconnaissance so he's up-to-date on who might be in our part of the world."

"Your dad is amazing. You couldn't have a better business partner."

"Well, we may not have any business left once we've been branded as the place Rachel and Buzz *didn't* get married. Maybe this is the curse of the Caddo well. The price I'm paying for tearing it down."

He could just imagine her lip poked out in an unusual bout of self-pity. It hadn't been too many hours since he'd been doing the same thing himself. Thank goodness his brother had been there to talk sense into him. Cullen had been right. Memories of their parents weren't attached to a place. They were held in the heart.

"Don't be silly. That mumbo jumbo was

just another tall Texas tale," Hunt comforted Gillian.

"That's an about-face," she said, perking up.

"It takes me a while. It's a man thing."

"Hunt, you had a sentimental tie to that well, didn't you?" she asked softly.

"I did. I camped out there after my folks died."

"Why didn't you tell me it was personal instead of playing it up as a legend?"

"Would it have made a difference?"

"I would have approached it differently. But hopefully when you see the waterfall that's going to be built where the well stood you'll have even more reason to appreciate the mansion."

"Then you did the right thing," he agreed.

"Can you forgive me for not being upfront with you?"

"Of course," he said, meaning it.

Alma would say he was finally growing up. His brothers would say it was about time!

Hunt's call-waiting beeped.

"Shouldn't you take that?" Gillian asked.

Hunt looked at the caller ID. "It's Robby. He'll leave me a message."

"Oh, no!" She groaned. "I bet he's already made air travel arrangements that can't be canceled. Everything is so expensive around Christmas. I'll either refund his costs or offer his family a free week's stay here to make it up to him."

"Don't add that to your list of stuff to fret over. Robby's a television rock star, and remember I told you he travels in one of those fancy motor coaches with room for his crew. It's all a write-off for his show, so don't give that cost any more worry."

"When were they expecting to be in Kilgore?"

"He plans to get on the road tomorrow, so they'll be in town the day after."

"Good, then there's still a chance we can stop them from leaving New York."

"If I know Robby, he'll want to come anyway and make a show out of it. He never passes up the chance to eat some Southwestern barbecue or Tex-Mex. Let me talk to him again when we hang up and see which way he leans. Maybe once he learns about Gabe, it'll seal the deal."

"But you haven't even talked to Gabe about this yet. How can you tell Robby it's all set up, if it isn't?"

"You leave that to me. When payback time comes, it may be painful, but you can bet your last buffalo nickel it'll be tasty."

"I can't believe you're taking this cancellation so lightly." Gillian sniffed.

"If you'd rather sit in the dirt and eat worms, you're going to be very lonely. I suspect that everybody else will get on board with the new game plan by the time I get home tomorrow evening."

"Are you in cahoots with my dad?" Her tongue was sounding fat.

"What makes you ask that?" Hunt chuckled at how easily Gillian was picking up Texas talk.

"He basically said the same thing when he told me I was paralyzed by shock, but that I'd see things differently in twenty-four hours."

"Are you still taking the pain meds?"

"Mom gave me another dose a little

while ago. I don't have any choice about taking them, when the alternative is a pounding knee."

"Well, that explains a lot. While your daddy and I are not presently in cahoots, I do agree that when I get home tomorrow, you'll have a different perspective on the circumstances."

"Hunt, what would I have done these past few months without you?"

"I'm fairly sure there would be a few more men in Kilgore with bleeding ulcers, but you'd have managed just fine."

"I'm serious. I owe so much to you. I don't want to do this without you, now or ever."

"Well, maybe you won't have to. We'll talk about it tomorrow."

"Hunt, I love you." Gillian's words were slurred.

"Is that you or the medication talking?"

"What medication?"

"Sleep tight, Gilly." He smiled to himself. And since she probably wouldn't remember his words, he put it on the line. "I love you too, my darling, and I intend to spend the rest of my life with you."

GILLIAN WOKE FEELING like the Russian army had marched through her mouth. Her tongue was thick and dry, and her lips were chapped from sleeping with her jaw hanging open. She had a headache that two aspirin would fix, but there was no longer a stabbing pain in her leg. She was thankful for that merciful blessing.

Still, she felt a vague sense of unease, the kind of foreboding the heroine in a scary film gets just before she passes into the dense forest.

Then Gillian remembered.

"The wedding is off." She said it out loud to help sort things clearly, without emotion. "Hunt comes home this afternoon. We have to figure out what to do with all the food and flowers because the deliveries will start today. And the installers will put up that enormous white tent to transform the terrace into a dining room and dance floor. What a waste."

"Good morning, baby girl." Her mother

knocked and then peeked around the door. "Look what the UPS driver just delivered."

She sat a carton on the bed and removed the top.

Gillian's breath caught in her throat as she lifted one of the brochures and slid her fingertips across the glossy cover.

"Oh, it's perfect." She leafed through the pages that she'd carefully proofed before they went to the printer. The photos were stunning, the anecdotes endearing. "What do you think he'll say?"

"He'll be speechless." Her mother settled on the mattress beside Gillian and draped an arm around her shoulders. "You've done the most amazing and selfless thing, and I don't believe Hunt has a clue about this decision. The Temple brothers, and probably the whole town, are going to be stunned when you reveal the marquee. You will be the darling of Kilgore."

Gillian shook her head. "That will depend on whether or not we survive and keep bringing jobs to town. But you and Dad know that being the belle of the ball had no bearing on my decision. It was simply the right thing to do. Once I realized that, I couldn't do otherwise and live with myself."

"Your dad and I are very proud of you." Her mom hugged her close. "Now, let's get you freshened up and downstairs. We don't have much time to figure out what to do with the food and flowers that are on the way. We can put the meat in the walk-in but all that produce will have to get used in the next few days. Maybe we can have another open house. We can use some of the flowers at the hotel if you decide to go the open house route, but we could also send some to local hospitals and assisted living centers."

Gillian waited until her mother stopped for breath before telling her about Hunt's backup plan.

"When did you speak with him?"

"Last night. It was about the time the pain medicine was kicking in, so I'm afraid I'm a bit fuzzy on the details, but he'll be home this afternoon, and we'll talk it all out then."

"Do you suppose you should reach out

to Rachel and give her one last opportunity to go through with her plans before we flip the wedding on its ear?"

"No, Mom, I don't believe I will. She has our number if she has a change of heart. But I'd imagine that by now the press is all over this story, and she's sick of hearing about it."

"Can't you just imagine Buzz cowering in fear of Rachel? I bet he's in the doghouse right now." Her mom giggled.

"It certainly won't be his first time. Though in the Hamptons, the dogs live better than ninety percent of the people in New York City, so I'm sure he'll survive."

"Are you girls covered up?" her father called from the hallway.

"Come on in, Dad."

"The stone masons are here. This is your last chance to change your mind. Once that monstrosity of a marquee has been assembled and cemented, it's there forever."

Gillian offered her father the brochure she had in her hand and smiled. "Go ahead and get the workers started. Mom and I already had that conversation, and I'm certain it's what I want to do."

She glanced back and forth between her parents, looking for signs of any concerns they hadn't shared with her.

"Do you two feel differently? This change impacts you, as well. I can still pull the plug and go with to the original plan. We'll have to reorder some items that have already been monogrammed, but the profit we're making for *not* hosting a high-end wedding more than covers that cost."

"Nope. This is your place, honey. We're just the bankers and the hired help. Your mother and I are actually enjoying the arrangement just as it is, and we don't want to take over executive decisions at this point, unless you ask us to. And even if you ask us, we reserve the right to say no!"

He smiled to convince her they were on board.

"Then please tell the crew to get busy, so the sign will be ready to be revealed the day after tomorrow."

"They're setting up a tent so they can work undercover."

"Perfect."

"I'll leave you girls to your personal business but don't take too long. It's almost ten o'clock and deliveries should begin by noon. We have a lot to figure out." He gave them both a peck on the cheek and left the room.

The hours passed too quickly. Gillian had every intention of putting on some makeup and taking her hair out of its ponytail before Hunt arrived, but the day got away from her. When somebody mentioned his Jeep was pulling up the drive, she was sitting beneath the enormous tent that now enclosed the terrace. She was surrounded by a mountain of fresh flowers that were being arranged on site, and she had her to-do list in her lap, still puzzling over how to shift their plans to match whatever Hunt had come up with overnight.

"Wow, look at this place!" Hunt called as he entered the tent. "If you'd brought me here blindfolded, I'd have no idea where I was."

"Then you understand just how I feel." A very handsome fortyish man with bleached hair followed Hunt as he made a beeline for where Gillian was sitting on a stool at one of the portable bars set up for what would have been the reception.

Hunt made quick work of taking in his surroundings, never slowing until he was at her side, taking her in his arms and covering her mouth with his. The kiss was brief but filled with promise.

"Goodness!" she exclaimed with a smile.

"As Mae West would say, 'Goodness has nothing to do with it.' I'm just glad to see my best girl."

My best girl? My best girl! It was the first time he'd ever made anything that might resemble a public overture. Maybe absence truly did make the heart grow fonder.

"Gabe, this is Gillian Moore, the owner of this incredible new boutique hotel, where you'll be vacationing with your family this summer. And, Gillian, this rascal is—"

"There's no need to introduce this man." She cut Hunt off. "Sir, I've had the pleasure of dining at a couple of your restaurants, and I've been watching you on television for years." She took the hand he offered and trusted he wouldn't notice hers had a case of the shakes.

He smiled warmly. "I hope you'll forgive me for crashing the gate like this without so much as a call ahead. But I happened to be free for a few days. My wife wanted to rest up from the holidays, and all my kids want to do is play with their video games. So when Hunt told me what was going on, I grabbed the bag that's always packed and headed to the airport with him. He assured me that you'd take an unexpected guest in stride."

"I'm a hotelier, so drop-ins are always welcome. And I've adjusted to so many things I hadn't expected since I moved to Texas that now 'the bigger, the better, and the more, the merrier' has become my philosophy. As it so happens we've recently had a cancellation, so there's a room available and ready for you."

"Yeah, Hunt brought me up to speed about that, but I'd already gotten the short version from Twitter. I'm sure it'll be on every entertainment news program tonight."

She hung her head. "Oh, do you really think so?"

"Yes, but that's exactly what we want! When Robby arrives tomorrow, and we reach out to the network together, you're going to have *Entertainment News* here in person."

"To cover what news event?" She still had no idea where this was headed.

"Let's get Gabe settled in his room, then we'll reconvene in the kitchen to strategize, while we sort through everything that got delivered today."

Hunt showed Gabe inside while Gillian hobbled to a nearby house phone to ask her dad to handle check-in duty since the staff was not scheduled to arrive until tomorrow.

Her mother caught her just as she hung up. "Honey, this just arrived by special messenger. It's for Rachel." Meredith held a large garment box with the name of a ritzy bridal boutique in New York as the return address. "Do you suppose it's her wedding dress?"

"I'm sure of it. She instructed me yesterday that I could keep it or toss it in the Dumpster. It made no difference to her. It's a custom design, so she can't take it back, and she doesn't want it in her possession."

The mother and daughter locked eyes and smiled.

"Shall we play dress up?" Meredith asked.

"Might as well."

"Oh, and one more thing."

Gillian sighed. "Give it to me straight."

"The wedding cake will be delivered at nine o'clock Friday morning."

"The wedding cake!" Gillian smacked the heel of her hand against her forehead. Yet another expensive detail that couldn't be canceled. "Mom, I have no idea what our cadre of chefs has come up with, but it better incorporate a twelve-hundred-dollar cake."

CHAPTER TWENTY-FOUR

THURSDAY WAS A blur in Gillian's mind.

Robby's incredible motor home cruised onto the property before daybreak. Eight people, including a cable network star, climbed out and never slowed down for the rest of the day. The hotel staff arrived, expecting to welcome a bridal party and instead *they* were welcomed by lights, cameras and action.

Gillian got a taste of reality television as people with video cameras climbed over banisters, furnishings and potted plants to get the best angle for each shot. Incredibly there wasn't a single sign they'd intruded on her space, and after a couple of hours, they seemed to fade into the wallpaper.

The kitchen was a different story. It had been transformed into a television studio where cameras were affixed to the ceiling and every corner of the work area to capture live food preparation. The three chefs hovered around the big pine table over endless cups of coffee and talked through the production they would tape the next day. The message of the show would be taking the sting out of a canceled wedding and turning the scene of the crime into a festive event.

Robby would throw down the gauntlet to Gabe and Hunt to transform the wedding menu, converting old standby dinner reception fare for a hundred guests into exciting, mouthwatering dishes that could only be found in top-rated restaurants.

And for dessert, they would each take a layer of the three-tiered cake and fashion it into something completely new. To complicate the challenge, each chef would come up with a personal theme for the sweet ending to his meal. And at the end, a crowd of locals would be invited to sample the dishes and declare one chef a winner.

Cullen had been recruited to round up the university's board of directors, who were all on winter break, and invite them to judge the meal. McCarthy was tasked with running down the mayor and city council members, and Joiner was expected to bring in acquaintances from the horsey set he ran with during polo season. Robby and Gabe had called a few friends from their cable network and put out the word that they were holding an event at the small hotel in East Texas where a secret celebrity wedding had been canceled. No names were mentioned but none were necessary.

The phone rang endlessly, all the rooms were booked, and the rented tables under the white tent for the next day's reception were reserved with standing room only. Gillian limped around as best she could, staying out of the way of fast-moving hand trucks and delivery personnel. The scent of hundreds of exotic flowers permeated the air, but tomorrow the aroma would change to garlic, onions and roasted meats.

The despair that had invaded Gillian's spirit on Christmas Day had been replaced with cautious optimism. If history was any indicator, a lot could still go wrong. But major-league talent was in charge of the recovery, and all she could do was hang on for dear life and enjoy the ride.

HUNT ARRIVED AT the mansion on Friday morning ready to rumble. He was in his element and in Pap's place. It was a wish come true, just not in the way he'd imagined or planned. Though that was to be expected, since he'd never done any planning. This wouldn't be happening if not for Gillian's dreams, and all the hard work she and her folks had done to turn those dreams into reality.

This day would be a one-of-a-kind experience that Hunt would never forget. And, if the opportunity presented itself, he had every intention of making it unforgettable for Gillian. But first he had to get through the challenge. The final show would be edited down to forty-eight minutes before airing, but the filming of the introduction, food prep, chef banter, judging and local color commentary would take up the better part of eight hours.

He entered through the tent and quickly glanced around. Gillian had directed the housekeeping staff and the floral design team in reworking the ostentatious wedding arrangements into tablescapes more suitable for a wintertime dinner party. He made a mental note of one more talent she had up her sleeve and then made a beeline for the kitchen where the love of his life was laughing with the camera crew.

"They won't let me send out for a box of Krispy Kreme."

"Of course not, this is a food set." Hunt nodded in understanding. "We'll have retakes and leftovers all day long. They don't want to spoil their appetites with doughnuts when there's likely to be beef Wellington in the next hour."

Gillian handed him a cup of coffee that he didn't have time to drink, but he deposited his knives on his workstation and took a sip to show his appreciation for her thoughtfulness.

"I presume from that Cheshire Cat smile that you're not even remotely nervous. The jitters have been gnawing at my insides since midnight," she admitted.

"Oh, no, I'm not worried about today.

This is gonna be nothin' but fun," Hunt assured Gillian. He began the ritual of unpacking and laying out the knives he would need for the day's competition. They were his secret weapons, his tools of the trade. Then he pulled a fresh chef's coat from his bag, slipped it over the T-shirt he'd worn beneath his jacket and buttoned it up.

"Chef, you look mighty handsome this morning." Gillian's eyes were shining.

"That means a lot coming from the prettiest girl at the party." While the others in the kitchen watched, he slipped his arms around Gillian's waist, pulled her close and captured her mouth. To the tune of whistles and catcalls, he gave her a sample of what was to come when the day was done. When the kiss ended, he kept his face close to hers for a private moment. "I should have asked permission for that public display of affection in your workplace, boss lady."

"This is your kitchen, Chef. In here you call all the shots."

"You make it awful hard for a man to want to work elsewhere."

"That's the plan. Now get busy and win

one for Temple Territory." With the help of her crutches, Gillian navigated past Robby's crew and out of sight.

"Temple Territory?" he mused under his breath. "I don't know if that was a mental relapse or a good luck charm, but either way, winning this one in the honorable name of Temple is just what I plan to do."

The cooking was well underway when the crowd started to pour onto the property to be the local cast for the show. The impromptu party atmosphere could be felt everywhere. When filming moved outdoors among the townspeople, they took to the script like regulars. Puns about runaway brides and grooms with cold feet erupted spontaneously, making for great television.

Robby was an expert at ad-libbing before the cameras, and he became the choir director leading the rowdy bunch of Texans in a chorus of jokes. Not to be outdone, Gabe came up with one funny story after another as he cooked, making it impossible to determine where the truth ended and the yarn-spinning began.

Hunt kept his focus on the food and let

the other chefs have the limelight. He'd gladly concede the popular vote as long as he took home the title for Temple Territory. Tonight, when the outdoor lights were turned up, Gillian would reveal her marquee and officially declare Moore House open for business. It was kind of her to let him have this last day in the kitchen while he could still think of it as Pap's place.

A ruckus outside announced newcomers. There was applause, laughter, chatter and then quiet as muffled voices spoke to the crowd. Then the loudest applause of the day so far broke out, and Hunt sensed the stakes had just been raised. Was there a chance Rachel and Buzz had shown up after all? Or had the governor in Austin heard about the goings-on over in Kilgore and decided to get some face time before the television cameras?

A blond head bobbed in the doorway of the crowded kitchen, and then Hunt noticed James wearing a wide grin. Yep, there had been an important turn of events, and they were trying to share the news.

"*Entertainment News* is here," somebody announced.

"It's about time," Robby and Gabe chorused without even looking up from their prep stations, never slowing from their work. "Who'd they send?"

"Some young correspondent," a familiar voice explained as the person edged through the overcrowded room. "Some fellow who was hanging out in New Orleans, and offered to drive over and give a little class to this story."

"Emilio, my friend!" Bobby called out. "I should have guessed it was you when the excitement outside didn't last long."

"Grab an apron, and we'll teach you how to make gumbo," Gabe taunted Emilio, a world-renowned chef from Louisiana.

Hunt hoped one day he'd earn the right to join in the irreverence that existed between these men. They were considered royalty, the "old-timers" in a television genre that had erupted in popularity during his adulthood.

Emilio laughed at their jabs. "We'll see if

you two have more to offer than talk after I've tasted your cooking."

He examined a fingerling potato that Hunt had painstakingly turned. "Nice cuts," Emilio complimented. "My money is on Team Temple." He patted Hunt on the shoulder and the nerves he'd told Gillian he wasn't feeling kicked into overdrive.

"Keep working, my friends, time is running out. There's a hungry mob under that tent waiting on the hors d'oeuvres course as we speak, and I'm about to join them. Don't disappoint us."

Hunt remembered that the competition on the reality show had been stiff, but this was another level of stress entirely. What had he been thinking to bring these food megastars to East Texas to annihilate him before a home crowd that included his family and the woman he hoped to marry?

GILLIAN HAD BELIEVED a celebrity wedding would be the perfect vehicle to put her hotel in the social spotlight. But what was going on within the confines of the property today had caused a bigger fuss and had brought more attention to the hotel than she could ever have imagined. And it was all thanks to the man who felt he'd let his family down by not making Pap Temple's mansion his own while he had the chance.

Gillian sat at the head table with her parents and Hunt's brothers to sample the meals the three incredible chefs had created. If it had been physically possible, she'd have kicked herself for not asking Hunt ahead of time about his menu, as the tasting was blind, the food served without the chefs in the room to present their meals. The diners would pick the winner without bias for their favorite celebrity chef.

Bless his heart, Emilio stepped up to act as the master of ceremonies as if he'd been invited for that purpose. He regaled the diners with stories of coming of age in television along with Robby and Gabe. He added how gratifying it was to welcome and mentor talented new chefs such as Hunt.

As evening fell, the food kept coming, and coming, and coming. One amazing dish after another was presented for tasting. The noisy diners became silent as they sampled and filled out the scorecards that were collected after each course.

"When those delivery trucks showed up, I figured we had enough food to feed Cox's Army. But I never dreamed there was so much variety among the volume. Seafood, beef, pork, every vegetable known to mankind…" Meredith observed, her cheeks puffed out as if she might explode.

"It drives home the point that you don't have to travel to Maine to enjoy fresh lobster or to California for the perfect wine pairing," James pointed out. "Gillian, your restaurant will have all the visibility you hoped for and should stay booked solid between *Entertainment News*'s immediate story and Robby's show that will air sometime next year."

"I haven't had time to tell you, but they're going to rush this episode through production, so it'll air in the summer to give brides-to-be some new ideas on what to serve at their receptions."

"And to give their fathers hope that the money won't be all for naught if the couple changes their mind." James raised a cheerful toast.

As if his raised glass was a cue, the lights dimmed, and the ceiling of the tent as well as the trees outside glowed to life with hundreds of thousands of tiny white lights. The setting was a perfect companion for the Texas night sky sprinkled with too many stars to count.

Emilio once again stepped to the microphone.

"And now for the pièce de résistance, dessert. No canceled wedding would be complete without a canceled wedding cake."

He paused for laughter as three serving carts were wheeled out.

"For the final portion of the competition, we're going to bend the rules a bit and let each chef share a personal story behind how he chose to reconstruct a layer of the bride's cake."

Robby told of the first trifle his mother had taught him to make, and how basic the ingredients had been but how he might never again eat anything as fulfilling as that arrangement of lady fingers made with his own hands. So he'd cut the wedding cake into bite-size pieces, soaked them in sherry, layered them over traditional English custard and topped them with berries and fresh whipping cream.

Gabe shared the story of the birth of his first son, and how, after many hours of labor and then a C-section, his wife was craving chocolate cake with fudge icing. The doctor hadn't wanted her to eat such heavy food right after having surgery, so Guy had gone home and made a dark chocolate mousse with whipped milk chocolate topping and crushed Oreo cookie sprinkles. So for his dessert he'd taken the chocolate layer of the wedding cake, crumbled it into the food processor with whipped cream to create a thick mousse and topped it with crushed peppermint bark intended as gifts for the wedding guests.

Gillian's hands were shaking for Hunt as he stood beside his cart waiting for his chance to speak. Instead of beginning when the spotlight was turned his way, he stepped out of the circle of attention and made his way toward the table where she sat with her parents.

"Please come with me," he instructed as he stepped behind her chair and helped her stand. He walked slowly beside Gillian, his hand cupped beneath one elbow as she navigated the packed room on her crutches, wondering why he hadn't mentioned this beforehand. It must have been an idea that occurred to him at the last minute.

"Ladies and gentlemen, may I present your hostess for this event and the owner of this incredible boutique hotel, Moore House, Ms. Gillian Moore."

When the applause died down, Emilio once again spoke into the microphone. "Cooking all day has fried your brain, my friend, and you misspoke. The name of this fine establishment is Temple Territory."

Hunt shook his head. Emilio was wrong. This would be terribly embarrassing for Gillian and disastrous for him at the exact moment he had something life-changing to ask. He'd correct the mistake immediately.

"With all due respect to you, the name of this hotel is Moore House."

"Not according to the brochure." Emilio held up a glossy pamphlet, and everyone else in the room did the same. "Or this." Emilio held up the cocktail napkin from beneath his drink, and everyone else in the room did the same. "Or that." Emilio nodded and a guest at a nearby table handed Hunt a freshly folded cloth napkin. Hunt shook it open and held it to the light. The white monogram against the white linen clearly read *Temple Territory*.

The same guest handed Hunt a copy of the brochure and a cocktail napkin and both confirmed what Emilio had said: the name of the property remained Temple Territory.

Hunt's raised eyes were brimming with tears.

Gillian held her breath, praying the timing of her surprise wasn't more than he could publicly accept, because he still had work to do.

And there was one last thing to be revealed.

He exhaled the emotion that seemed about to overtake him, glanced one last time at the items that bore his family name, and then laid them on a nearby table. He reached both open palms toward Gillian, and she eagerly slipped her hands into his.

"All day long I assumed I was the one with a secret." He tipped his head toward the dessert on his cart. "I hate to throw a competition, but as you can see, my layer still looks like the top of a wedding cake. It was baked with the finest ingredients, iced with tender care and decorated with yellow roses, a symbol of strength, courage and enduring love in our great state. I couldn't tear this cake apart when it should be used for the purpose it was intended, to celebrate timeless and unending love."

Hunt went down on one knee, and the room erupted. If Gillian hadn't had crutches to lean on she'd have collapsed on the floor beside him.

"I don't have a ring to offer you right now, Gilly. But only because I know you and you'll want to pick it out yourself."

The crowd broke into laughter when she nodded agreement. She couldn't squeeze words past the lump in her throat.

"And you don't have to answer me on the spot, because we haven't even discussed this, and you'll want time to think it over. And you may not be too crazy about me asking you with the eyes of Texas watching."

Again he was right, and again she smiled and nodded, unable to speak.

"But if you would consider being my bride and letting me be your executive chef for the rest of our lives, you would make me a very happy cowboy."

The first whoops came from Hunt's brothers and Gillian's parents. When Cooper added his bark of approval, the rest of the makeshift ballroom joined in the celebration.

CHAPTER TWENTY-FIVE

HUNT HELD GILLIAN close to shield her from
the December wind. At the entrance to the
property, the family gathered in the dark.
His brothers, Gillian's father and Felix
tugged the cover loose and lifted it free
from the Texas-size stone marquee. Spot-
lights hit the new landmark from every direction, and the small group caught their
collective breath.

TEMPLE TERRITORY was deeply
etched into the finest Texas limestone, and
the centuries-old rocks that had once been
the exterior of the well were embedded in
the base of the marquee and would forever
remain part of Temple Territory.

The Caddo Nation protesters erupted in
applause.

"I love you, Gillian Moore."

"Because of Temple Territory?"

"In spite of it. You made me angry, and

then you made me crazy, and then you made me see the light of day. You're perfect for me. I adore you. I can't wait to make you my wife."

"I love you, too, Hunt Temple."

"Because I want to stay?"

"In spite of that. You fought with me, and then you mentored me, and then you showed me I can trust you with anything. Even my heart. Hunt, with you I can be who I am, only a better version. We're good together, and as long as your offer still stands, we'll have the very first wedding at Temple Territory."

Hunt pulled Gillian closer and showed her with his kiss that he never intended to let her go again.

"It's strange, but this is not the way I pictured finding love. I always thought I'd work on my career and then later make the time for a relationship."

Gillian's confession was almost an apology, but Hunt understood exactly how she felt.

"I believe it was King Soloman who said,

'In his heart a man plans his course, but the Lord determines his steps.'"

"How true," she agreed.

"We'll make our plans together from this day forward, Gillian. With divine help, our forever will go on between us and not around us." Back up on the hill, beneath the huge tent, a country band struck up an Irish reel to celebrate Robby's win.

Hunt hardly noticed as he held Gillian close and hummed a Texas two-step in her ear.

* * * * *

REQUEST YOUR FREE BOOKS!

2 FREE INSPIRATIONAL NOVELS
PLUS 2
FREE
MYSTERY GIFTS

Love Inspired®

YES! Please send me 2 FREE Love Inspired® novels and my 2 FREE mystery gifts (gifts are worth about $10). After receiving them, if I don't wish to receive any more books, I can return the shipping statement marked "cancel." If I don't cancel, I will receive 6 brand-new novels every month and be billed just $4.74 per book in the U.S. or $5.24 per book in Canada. That's a savings of at least 21% off the cover price. It's quite a bargain! Shipping and handling is just 50¢ per book in the U.S. and 75¢ per book in Canada.* I understand that accepting the 2 free books and gifts places me under no obligation to buy anything. I can always return a shipment and cancel at any time. Even if I never buy another book, the two free books and gifts are mine to keep forever.

105/305 IDN F49N

Name _____ (PLEASE PRINT)

Address _____ Apt. #

City _____ State/Prov. _____ Zip/Postal Code

Signature (if under 18, a parent or guardian must sign)

Mail to the Harlequin® Reader Service:
IN U.S.A.: P.O. Box 1867, Buffalo, NY 14240-1867
IN CANADA: P.O. Box 609, Fort Erie, Ontario L2A 5X3

**Are you a subscriber to Love Inspired books
and want to receive the larger-print edition?
Call 1-800-873-8635 or visit www.ReaderService.com.**

* Terms and prices subject to change without notice. Prices do not include applicable taxes. Sales tax applicable in N.Y. Canadian residents will be charged applicable taxes. Offer not valid in Quebec. This offer is limited to one order per household. Not valid for current subscribers to Love Inspired books. All orders subject to credit approval. Credit or debit balances in a customer's account(s) may be offset by any other outstanding balance owed by or to the customer. Please allow 4 to 6 weeks for delivery. Offer available while quantities last.

Your Privacy—The Harlequin® Reader Service is committed to protecting your privacy. Our Privacy Policy is available online at www.ReaderService.com or upon request from the Harlequin Reader Service.
We make a portion of our mailing list available to reputable third parties that offer products we believe may interest you. If you prefer that we not exchange your name with third parties, or if you wish to clarify or modify your communication preferences, please visit us at www.ReaderService.com/consumerschoice or write to us at Harlequin Reader Service Preference Service, P.O. Box 9062, Buffalo, NY 14269. Include your complete name and address.

LIDIR13R

REQUEST YOUR FREE BOOKS!

2 FREE INSPIRATIONAL NOVELS
PLUS 2
FREE
MYSTERY GIFTS

Love Inspired

HISTORICAL
INSPIRATIONAL HISTORICAL ROMANCE

REQUEST YOUR FREE BOOKS!

2 FREE CHRISTIAN NOVELS
PLUS 2
FREE
MYSTERY GIFTS

HEARTSONG
PRESENTS

YES! Please send me 2 Free Heartsong Presents novels and my 2 FREE mystery gifts (gifts are worth about $10). After receiving them, if I don't wish to receive any more books I can return the shipping statement marked "cancel." If I don't cancel, I will receive 4 brand-new novels every month and be billed just $4.24 per book in the U.S. and $5.24 per book in Canada. That's a savings of at least 20% off the cover price. It's quite a bargain! Shipping and handling is just 50¢ per book in the U.S. and 75¢ per book in Canada.* I understand that accepting the 2 free books and gifts places me under no obligation to buy anything. I can always return a shipment and cancel at any time. Even if I never buy another book, the two free books and gifts are mine to keep forever.

159/359 HDN FVYK

Name	(PLEASE PRINT)	

Address		Apt. #

City	State	Zip

Signature (if under 18, a parent or guardian must sign)

Mail to the **Harlequin® Reader Service:**
IN U.S.A.: P.O. Box 1867, Buffalo, NY 14240-1867

* Terms and prices subject to change without notice. Prices do not include applicable taxes. Sales tax applicable in N.Y. This offer is limited to one order per household. Not valid for current subscribers to Heartsong Presents books. All orders subject to credit approval. Credit or debit balances in a customer's account(s) may be offset by any other outstanding balance owed by or to the customer. Please allow 4 to 6 weeks for delivery. Offer available while quantities last. Offer valid only in the U.S.

Your Privacy—The Harlequin® Reader Service is committed to protecting your privacy. Our Privacy Policy is available online at www.ReaderService.com or upon request from the Harlequin Reader Service.
We make a portion of our mailing list available to reputable third parties that offer products we believe may interest you. If you prefer that we not exchange your name with third parties, or if you wish to clarify or modify your communication preferences, please visit us at www.ReaderService.com/consumerschoice or write to us at Harlequin Reader Service Preference Service, P.O. Box 9062, Buffalo, NY 14269. Include your complete name and address.

ReaderService.com

Manage your account online!

- Review your order history
- Manage your payments
- Update your address

*We've designed
the Harlequin® Reader Service
website just for you.*

Enjoy all the features!

- Reader excerpts from any series
- Respond to mailings and special monthly offers
- Discover new series available to you
- Browse the Bonus Bucks catalog
- Share your feedback

Visit us at:
ReaderService.com